Hillbilly Godfather

Hillbilly Godfather

Printed in the United States of America

ISBN: 978-0-9863992-9-9
Library of Congress Control Number: 2026906100

Cover art and interior illustrations
by Ruth Hawkins, created with ChatGPT (OpenAI),
AI-generated imagery.

Hillbilly Godfather

A Novella by
Van Hawkins

Writers Bloc
Jonesboro, Arkansas

Also by Van Hawkins

Hampton and Newport News. A Pictorial History. 1975

Dorothy and the Shipbuilders of Newport News. 1976

The Historic Triangle. An Illustrated History of Jamestown, Williamsburg and Yorktown, 1980

Plowing New Ground. The Southern Tenant Farmers Union and its Place in Delta History. 2007

Duty Bound. The Hyatt Brothers and Confederates of the Third Arkansas Infantry Regiment, Army of Northern Virginia, C.S.A. 2011

Horizons. A Novel. 2012

Smoke Up the River. Steamboats and the Arkansas Delta. 2016

Moaning Low: From Slavery to Peonage. Involuntary Servitude in the Arkansas Delta. 2019

A New Deal in Dyess. The Depression Era Agricultural Resettlement Colony in Arkansas. 2015, expanded 2020

The Colonel's Clay. A Novel. 2020

Unbearable Things. A Novel. 2021

Cries from the Walls. Hell in Arkansas Prisons. 2024

With thanks to Rob Lamm
for his sound advice
and my wife Ruth
for her editorial assistance

Doss Family Tree

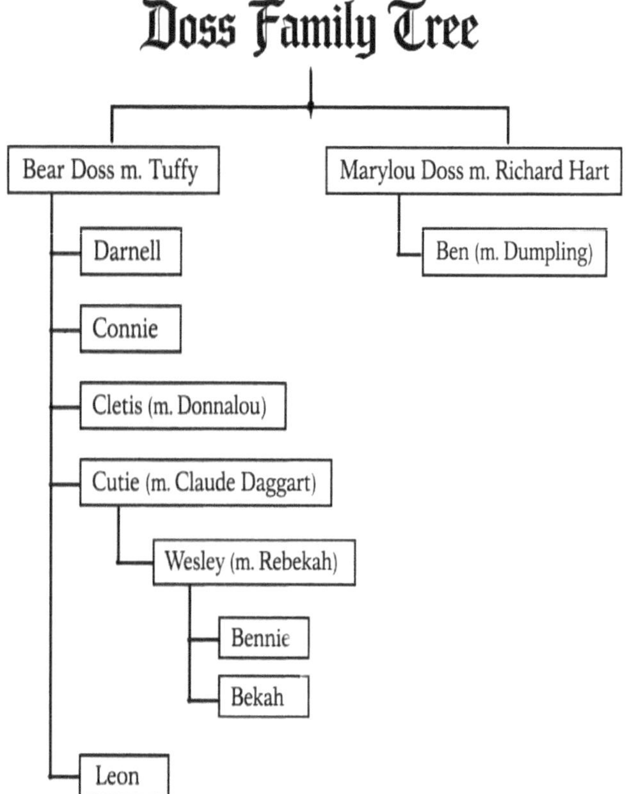

Contents

Ben Abandoned

Richard dropped off his son Ben near dark at his Aunt Tuffy's and Uncle Bear's house a day after his mom abandoned them. Richard wanted to run off too but lost his driver's license after three DUIs. Bear's sister Marylou, Ben's mom, was a Doss, and kin couldn't be turned away. While the boy sat on a bench eyeballing the fading cypress floor in the Doss home, Bear saw the shame and patted Ben's head twice. He then slumped into a worn-out recliner to search for meaning in the funny papers. Only the television broke their silence, its rabbit ears adjusted to tune in a Billy Graham special from some Godforsaken African country. Bickering among Ben's five cousins usually filled the room, but only his wastrel cousin Darnell was around, and he was bad company. He had collapsed on the couch, high as a giraffe's ass after taking two capsules of unknown drugs. He had swapped them for five antifreeze jugs he stole from an auto parts store. Connie and Cletis were in the hog barn turning a sow into sausage. Cutie and Leon were elsewhere entertained.

Tuffy, wearing a sweaty gray t-shirt and tan shorts, checked on Ben now and then while baking scratch biscuits. She told him to go out and ask Connie if he needed anything. What Ben didn't know then was she made Connie his permanent keeper.

Tuffy and Bear met many years ago while clinging to grimy steel monkey bars at a church playground after Sunday School. Bear grew into a big boy with curly black hair. He liked Tuffy's looks and spunk and asked her to go into some bushes near the creek and play doctor. But she wasn't having it. Tuffy threatened to gut-stomp him if he said another word about it. Since Bear's kin had been tree cutters for decades his family soon moved to distant hills not yet cut over. The day before he moved Bear told

Tuffy he was sorry for the way he acted. She thought better of him after that. When Bear turned 17 he joined the Marines, and after boot camp and infantry training he ended up digging trenches and building roads and barracks in the Philippines. His platoon patrolled but never saw rebels worth killing.

When Bear returned home he found the hill where his family was cutting and helped for a while. But Bear walked away when he heard that a lumber mill in Grinder's Switch needed help. Another reason he came was to marry Tuffy if she would have him. His first day back Bear learned about Tuffy's predicament. The bank's owner had an arrogant son obsessed with Tuffy's large bosoms. The punk copped a feel whenever he passed by. The boy learned from his father that Tuffy's family was behind on their loans. This led the boy to assume he could fondle them for free. After she warned him, he dared her to do something about it. She did something at the soda shop. Tuffy stomped his ass flat on the concrete floor. He had Converse imprints on his skinned head and cried like a baby before she let him up. That was the day her name changed from Margie to Tuffy.

The boy's rich daddy, Horace, controlled the school board. Members owed his bank money and struggled to pay it back. So members ruled Tuffy posed a danger to school kids and expelled her. After Bear found out what happened he searched for Horace Jr. who came home on weekends from a private school in Little Rock. The quivering boy faced Bear eyeball to eyeball on Main Street. Several folks passing by heard Bear's threat: "If I ever see you in town again I'll empty your toolbox."

The bank owner and his sniveling son went to Judge Wild Bill Cody to demand that he make the town marshal arrest Bear. But Horace misjudged Judge Cody, a cantankerous character who understood the law his way. Horace's demands had barely begun when Judge Cody interrupted: "First of all, Horace, you can't arrest a man for giving a spoiled kid good advice. If Bear finds out you're pestering me about this he may empty your toolbox too. We all know what this brat did to Tuffy and that you ended her education and future prospects out of revenge. You'd have to bribe a jury to win against Bear, and I'll not let that happen."

"Well then. What am I supposed to do?"

"I reckon they're all bad choices. You can send this boy to reform school where he belongs. You can let Bear saw off his privates on Main Street. Or you can all run off. I'm sure somebody will pay good money for your bank."

"You're crazy," Horace said.

"Funny you should say that. It's exactly what my wife Sweet Mama says when she can't get her way. Now ya'll get out of here so I can get ready for court." Horace sold the bank and bought a bankrupt savings and loan in Abilene, Texas.

Bear and Tuffy cuddled and kissed for a few weeks until they got married after her family binned their corn crop. Bear went to work for the lumber company, and the couple settled into a clapboard rent house. Bear planned to buy and enlarge the house when they got kids. That didn't take long. Darnell emerged headfirst during breach birth with stringy black hair, snake eyes and seeds of a sociopath embedded in his defective brain. He would grow into a big boy who learned little in school beyond how to lie, cheat, steal and fight dirty.

Connie grew up looking good, but skinny, nail hard and fearless. She agreed to assist Darnell with homework if he taught her how to fight low-down. This he did at night in the barn. Connie sometimes limped out, skinned up, bruised and dirty. Darnell showed her how to use knees, teeth, nails and knives and hit the mark with a pistol and 12-gauge. Ben later would benefit because Connie taught him what she learned, but she insisted he hide this stuff unless it was his only way out the door.

Bear and Tuffy had a kid every couple of years, give or take. Cletis came and went to farming early on. He followed Bear's giant steps across a field by jumping from one planted furrow to the next to avoid muddy middles. When he gave out Bear carried Cletis until he squirmed to be put back on his feet. Cletis earned good marks in school but disliked being there. It reduced his hours with the sun and warm soil. Everyone knew Cletis would shoulder the load when Tuffy and Bear said so.

They were pleased to have another girl when Cutie was born. But she didn't stay girly for long. Cutie grew up fast and clever. Figured out men would pay a premium if they wanted something bad enough. So she went into sales. Cutie grew into a Playboy Bunny figure with blonde hair. Her soft southern accent gave men a lot to think about. Kept her in control. Kept them hopeful. When Cutie sold makeup, women bought it to help them look a little like her. If she sold men's cologne, the Old Spice shelf emptied. Reading tells and closing deals fast came natural.

Leon looked like a wet weasel when he squeezed into the real world. Soon his darting eyes and wrinkled nose convinced everyone he couldn't be trusted. Leon verified this by choosing Uncle Fred Doss to be his mentor. Uncle Fred sold used cars to poor folks who couldn't get credit elsewhere. He financed purchases at shylock rates and foreclosed if car loans went an hour overdue. Leon learned how to get along by legally stealing money.

Ben's mom Marylou and dad Richard Hart, a modest man with thin brown hair and round tortoise shell glasses, met in a literature survey class. Both called themselves English majors and arranged their schedules to attend many of the same classes. She allowed Richard to put this arm around her waist during walks to the malt shop. Both graduated in three years and married. The wedding came about only after he agreed to live in the hills with her. Marylou was a Doss with blood that ran too thick and deep. Richard suspected she was hiding a lot inside her but didn't see it until too late. She taught in Grinder's Switch's high school. Richard at a nearby junior college.

Marylou's brother Bear found a house for them. Richard made an acceptable offer and borrowed their downpayment from his family. The two-story wood and stone house rested in a stand of cottonwood trees on a small hill near Grinder's Switch. The town of a few hundred grew up on hard dirt and gravel in the hills. Roving Doss kin founded the town, which created and continued its disreputable reputation. No one knew where those people came from, but church folks assumed that where they were going would be flaming hot. At night Marylou and Richard graded student papers until bedtime. On weekends she watched soap operas.

He converted a small room into an office and lived there. They hardly said a word to each other. Richard read extensively and wrote literary articles submitted to scholarly publications that rejected them. Neither visited kin because Richard couldn't abide them. This changed when Ben was born. Tuffy came to the hospital and helped bring him home. Marylou remained indifferent.

Richard, too, until Ben grew old enough to become a tutorial project. From *Winnie the Pooh* through *Waiting for Godot* he tutored Ben intensely in art and its ways. Harshly, because Richard didn't like Ben. Partly because Ben had been designed for exceptions, not rules. Tuffy didn't like the pressure Richard applied but didn't consider it her place to step in. Under his father's tutelage Ben became immersed in literature, history and philosophy. Cutie came and went. Treated him to cheeseburgers and milkshakes. Their conversations mostly concerned her weight, complexion and wealthy prospects. Cutie usually slipped him some cash for what she called odds and ends, along with a warning to never let Darnell or Leon see it.

Connie observed silently. But Ben saw her backbone on a church hayride during Vacation Bible School run by Southern Baptist deacons. During religion classes deacons terrorized boys with descriptions of a road to Hell littered with empty beer cans. A path flooded with people who drank, gambled and slow danced too close at the prom.   Pre-marital sex led to knocked-up girlfriends and the clap. Masturbation caused large finger warts despite abundant evidence to the contrary.

During a hayride that Connie took with Ben a group of older boys threw bales at smaller kids. One almost knocked Ben off the trailer. Connie yelled: "You gobs of vomit stop that shit, or I'll stop it for you." Connie directed it at Willard, a town bully.

Willard yelled back: "Shut up you Doss bitch, or we'll kick you off."

"Well, start kickin'."

When Willard stepped toward her Connie pulled out a hand-rolled Prince Albert from her bra and a long kitchen match. She lit the match with a fingernail and marched toward him. "Tell you what, Willard, how 'bout I throw this match in that clump of hay at your feet. Let's see how long the fire takes to lick your sweet meat. Shouldn't be but a second or two. You'll know when they start to crackle."

Willard blinked, swallowed hard and shuffled backward. She followed with the match until he fell off the trailer onto his empty head. Connie then headed toward the other boys. They jumped off and began a long walk back to church with a wobbly Willard.

Ben said, "I'm sorry, Connie. I should've backed you."

"Didn't need it. Willard just found out never to fuck with somebody crazier than you are."

Ben didn't like going to Bible School or anywhere else. People said: "How are you doing? If you need to talk just let me know." He avoided school counselors and county nurses who sought to share advice from manuals about disturbed kids. People took withdrawal to be a result of trauma. Maybe it was. But he owned it. Not them. Besides, he was depending on characters in books he read. Tough men. Too cold to care about anything.

The beautyshop claimed Marylou fell for a brawny timber cutter. He caught her eye when she was home alone watching him chainsaw bare chested near the house. A woman in the shop getting a perm and color saw her riding out of town in his pickup with her arm around his tattooed shoulders. Tuffy put the word out that if anyone learned where Marylou was to let her know the location. She would settle up with both of them the hard way.

Richard picked up Ben after a couple of drunken weeks following his mom's departure. He lived on Camels and vodka. Ben got by on Homer. He stayed with his dad a lot but preferred hitching a ride with Cutie or Connie to their house and staying until Richard ordered him home. Tuffy made growing up easy in some ways and hard in others. At first she took him to church where a preacher swore a loving God would never let him down. But God already had. Ben's disgruntled five cousins sat in a row on the same pew. Antsy as naughty sparrows perched on a low branch.

Ben stopped paying attention when preachers told him to take all his troubles to Jesus. Jesus never did a damn thing about them so why bother. Scandals amused him. Church ladies suspected the married choir leader had too many private sessions with Nadine, his piano player. Ben overheard Tuffy talking to them about it at the grocery store. The women, eyebrows raised and lips puckered, wondered if Nadine would admit to the congregation that she fornicated with a married man and resign. Ben told Tuffy: "I don't know much about anything. But I know that ain't gonna happen." It didn't. The Women's Auxiliary had to spin a prayer wheel to save Nadine's soul.

Thanks to Cletis and Connie, Ben earned a full hand's wages by the time he was 15. Tuffy made Leon loan him a beat-up pickup from Uncle Fred's lot, which Leon now managed.

Leon argued for money to rent the truck until Tuffy told him to shut up or she'd charge for room and board while he was in between women. Leon read her mind and recognized he now had to supply Ben with a better vehicle every other year. Tuffy would keep count. Cletis became Ben's role model. He lived quietly. Almost entirely within himself. Dry as burned toast. But determination and focus always pulled him through. Ben tried to help Cletis slop but often threw up in the bucket since the smell sickened him. "You better keep readin' them books, buddy. You'll never make a hog farmer." Advice Ben accepted.

Women Troubles

Cutie had shared a duplex with several women on the lookout for men to cover their overdrafts. But she moved into a nice apartment after landing her perfect job. The barbershop rated Cutie's body a 10. After she got a job at the Country Club bar the cash drawer filled up on her shifts. Cutie's full lips in a shade of red always smiled. She seemed close, but never reachable. Cutie pocketed huge tips. After last call over-served men watched through a window as Cutie hiked up her skirt to kick-start a used Harley she bought with bar money. Claude Daggart, a wealthy older fellow, enjoyed watching Cutie's round butt bounce when she kicked. Daggart owned a 12,000-acre spread, more or less. It grew enough corn and hay to feed hundreds of cattle. He expanded sideways and owned several businesses that sold farm supplies and equipment. His wife Lucille was an untamed shrew with a screw loose and an ass that fell a foot after her cheerleader days. The barbershop said Claude had a ride on the side already but was shopping for a new model. Daggart offered Cutie cash, jewelry and a night in Vegas, but no sale.

After he became besotted and begged Cutie for at least a one-off, she closed the deal. Cutie took him down in a Peabody Hotel suite in Memphis. "I hope you liked all the stuff I did for you," she said while adjusting her black thong in front of him. "'cause none of it'll never happen again. Don't call or come near me till I hear the four words you got to say next."

"What are those?"

"Will you marry me?"

When Cutie strutted out smiling Daggart realized that lust was trump in her game. After being shunned repeatedly he made an appointment with his accountant and attorney to start hiding assets from his wife's divorce attorney. Daggart always cooked his books to short the IRS, so this was a lay-up. He filed and Cutie got a one-carat engagement ring and a confirmed wedding date.

Leon also had woman troubles when Miss Netttie pulled into the car lot in an old Pontiac he sold her two days earlier. The front door sounded cranky as she struggled to climb out. "Fine day, isn't it. What can I do for you Miss Nettie?"

"Give me a new hubcap. Look at that back wheel. The hubcap flew off and rolled into Blue Hole ditch."

"Can't buy a new one. Wouldn't look right. The other three are old. Tell you what. Fish it out of Blue Hole. I'll put it back on. No charge. How 'bout that, huh?"

Miss Nettie swung her big purse hard. It busted his nose and turned his eyeballs into red marbles. "Goddamn you," Leon roared and rolled over on his stomach to protect his private parts. "I'll have you arrested."

"Try that, and I'll be back with a butcher's knife. Settle it that-a-way."

Still, Leon drove to the jail and complained to the marshal. "That old woman's got sand up her ass. She looked the car over before buyin' it. It's not my fault she's half blind. And it's not my place to talk down stuff I'm sellin'." Leon pulled out the handkerchief he stuffed in his nose. Blood leaked out. "Look here. I'm still bleedin'. My eyeballs may pop out."

Marshal Coldman leaned back in his office chair with screaming springs before delivering the bad news. "Look here, Leon. I'm not arrestin' Miss Nettie. She's 90 years old, give or take. I'm not puttin' her in jail. Work it out between you."

"How?"

"Don't know. But I'm not gonna arrest 'er. The whole town would vote me out next election."

"She's got to have insurance, don't she?"

"Couldn't get tags without it. Don't know if she's got a license. Don't wanna know. I told my deputies not to stop her unless she runs over something and it stops breathin'."

"I'm gonna have big bills comin' from my chiropractor. I may even have a brain stroke. I'll need a lot of money to pay for all her adjustments."

"I never heard of a policy rider that covers gettin' hit in the head by a crazy woman."

"What're you gonna do if she comes after me with a butcher's knife?"

"After we bury you I'll charge her with murder if we can prove it."

Fortunately for the marshal his radio squawked. A fat farmer fell into a cistern north of town, and his crippled wife couldn't pull him out. She called for help. The marshal put his hat on and suggested Leon buy another hubcap. "It might save your life." That's how it got worked out.

Ben's life seemed okay, by and large, but Darnell insisted it lacked a girlfriend with little willpower. His romantic advice to Ben was simple: "Girls are sittin' on what they're selling so get 'em on their back with their legs in the air as fast as you can. Don't buy it. Just rent it for a while." This advice proved to be useless when Sara Lynn, a cousin, caught Ben's attention between classes. She worked part-time washing hair in the beautyshop and knew who wanted what and how bad. "Do you know Pene wants you to ask her out?"

"Penelope?"

"Yeah. You ain't got a clue, do you Sherlock."

"Are you sure?"

She laughed and walked away.

Pene was a year younger than Ben. Bright, blunt and attractive. They had exchanged greetings a few times, but he hardly knew her. A secret reason he wanted the date was to show off his current ride. A black and white '57 Ford Fairlane. Tuffy told Leon the loan might last a while so he couldn't sell it. Leon bitched about it incessantly.

Ben grinned big when Cutie handed him the keys. "Is it mine to drive whenever?"

"Sure is, Sweetie. Here's a twenty for your first fill-up and date."

"No wonder Leon is mad at me."

"What are you talkin' about?"

"I heard Leon is mad at me for takin' his car."

"Who told you that?"

"Everybody."

Her face went from peaches and cream to purple. "Did he say somethin' to you?"

"No."

"Don't you worry, Sweetie. Connie and I'll have a sit-down with that greasy runt."

They did. Leon told Ben afterward to keep the car as long as he wanted.

After several anxiety attacks Ben followed Pene out the school's front door and onto a dead grass path to the street.

She turned. "Are you following me?"

"Yep."

"Why?"

"I want to ask if I can walk you home, but I'm afraid you'll say no."

"Are you askin'?"

"Yep."

"Then I'm sayin' yes."

They walked about two miles to her family's large brick rancher just outside the city limits. He entertained her by mimicking the coach's deplorable grammar while teaching civics. Pene's family lived on a section of mixed dirt raising corn and hay. But most of their money came from a large cattle operation. Her folks did all the work and became financially successful and respected throughout the county.

After reaching the front gate he got up the gumption to ask: "Will you go to the movie with me Friday night?"

"What is it?"

"*Splendor in the Grass*, with Natalie Wood and Warren Beatty. It's supposed to be good."

"Okay. But two things first. I'll not ride with anyone who is drinking. Two, if you try to make me do something I don't want to, I'll slap you till your teeth fall out."

"No problem. I only drink and smoke reefer with Darnell. And I don't want to roam the hills a toothless vagabond looking for a blind date."

"Oh my. You're as quick as they say. And I can already tell you're a mess."

Both liked the movie. And their opinions filled the ride home, along with the elephant. Country kids usually ended dates on dirt roads juggling body parts. But he couldn't decide what to say about that. Pene made it easy. "If you want we can park on the road by my house and talk for a while."

"I'd like that."

"Daddy doesn't want me on a dirt road in the middle of nowhere with some sticky-fingered boy."

"A wise man." After several long seconds: "Is it okay if I ask you out again?"

"Of course. But if we start going out, never lie to me. If I catch you lyin' it's over forever. And don't try to push me into anything intimate. That's my call."

"Okay. But after you fall for me can we get buck nekkid and have some fun?"

Pene held both hands over her face to hide. "Oh lord. What have I got myself into," she said behind her fingers. Then to him: "Why did you take me to see that movie? Was it because of the emotional damage sexual repression did to the girl?"

"No. The screenplay is by William Inge, a gifted playwright I admire. And the title comes from one of my favorite Wordsworth poems:

> *Our birth is but a sleep and a forgetting:*
> *The soul that rises with us, our life's Star,*
> *Hath had elsewhere its setting,*
> *And cometh from afar: …*
> *What though the radiance which was once so bright*
> *Be now for ever taken from my sight,*
> *Though nothing can bring back the hour*
> *Of splendour in the grass, of glory in the flower;*
> *We will grieve not, rather find*
> *Strength in what remains behind.*

After quoting those lines from memory he looked at Pene. Her cheeks were moist. Pene wiped her eyes and sniffled. "I better go. Daddy knows you've got Doss blood. He might be waiting at the front door to see if my blouse is ripped and my skirt is hiked up. If he sees me crying, he'll come after you with a cattle prod. But Ben, never lose track of who you are deep inside. Never let that go." She leaned over and lightly kissed him on the lips, but her eyes promised more.

They soon grew close, appreciating the time and comfort shared watching movies, studying together, swapping stories and eating greasy cheeseburgers. He enjoyed walking with her among animals in their pasture. Pene had adopted a wandering doe and young fawn with beautiful big eyes. She cared for them like a mother would. Ben warned Pene to never read *The Yearling*. It would break her heart.

Parked on a sultry night many months later Pene became restless. After a sensuous kiss she said, "I know you're frustrated. And I know from living with two older brothers for many years how that turns out for the girl." She paused, but he left the hole to see how she filled it. "I know how much you want me, but I'm not ready, Ben. I don't want to lose you so please wait." He became patient after such fierce honesty about what in those days good girls didn't admit. He waited until she stopped whispering no.

Pene had been locked out of the space inside Ben where he stored his secrets. During their many talks Pene gently urged him to let her in. "I don't talk about that stuff to anybody," he said. "Most people wear masks to hide who they really are and what they want. You can't trust anybody. You're an exception. But it's too much to ask."

"I know why you're hurt so bad," Pene said, "but I come from a better place. Maybe over time we can make you a better place. I can't figure out why your mom ran off with that redneck and hurt you like this."

"Well, maybe love ain't blind, just entirely self-centered. Connie told me she would settle up if I wanted, but I said no. Pene, please drop it." So she did.

Despite their expanding affection Pene slapped Ben when the carnival came to town. Its sleazy hustlers set up in the town ballpark, and crowds rushed to see its sights. Pene arranged for Ben to take her and meet her cousin Karen and her date Lonnie. While strolling through the tawdry Midway they came to the Ferris wheel. They wanted to hop on, but not Ben. "I'm terrified of heights," he said. "That wheel looks like it belongs in Leon's junk pile. The man running the thing hasn't been sober in a year or two." They insisted, but he refused.

Pene got mad and climbed aboard with the others. The thing cranked up amid a loud clanking. When they neared the top, a deafening bang stopped their ascent. Packed seats swayed with frantic faces. Some screamed. Some cussed. Southern Baptists prayed for intervention by a white protestant Jesus. When the operator got his machine running it made a slow descent with metal clawing metal. People on seats near the ground jumped off. Even old people with hip problems. Chaos from top to bottom struck Ben as humorous, and he laughed. Several people having walking nervous breakdowns glared at him. Pene hit the ground running, straight at him. She slapped Ben hard.

"What was that about?"

"We were up there scared shitless, and you started laughing at us."

"No, no, no. You were too far away to see that I was praying for you. I prayed to God that we would meet again in Heaven." Pene wound up, but Ben caught her hand. "Don't hit me again. It hurts." She refused to ride home with him. No clutching under tree limbs. No tongue-diving kisses. Nothing.

Darnell hadn't heard the Ferris wheel commotion. He was in a crowded carnival tent watching a hermaphrodite dance naked for five dollars a ticket.

Ben lost Pene because of Darnell and her unequivocal rejection of liars. It started with the fact that he owed Darnell for liquor and other stuff furnished over many years. Darnell fancied a hairdresser named Marline that he met in a juke joint in the next county. She agreed to go out with him but only on a double date. Darnell made it clear that Ben's bar bill had arrived and it was settling up time. He lied to Pene, telling her he would be at a poetry reading in Little Rock. Late that afternoon Darnell cranked up a bleached white Mercury Marauder with rust-colored primer patches that Leon rented him for the night. The trip took a turn for the worse when Ben met his date at Marline's beautyshop. She looked like Janis Joplin, did not want to go and probably was 20 years older than him. When they pulled into a spot at the drive-in Darnell rolled down the window and hooked on a speaker. He tried to get his tongue between Marline's clenched teeth before Janet Leigh spotted Bates Motel on the big screen.

When a wave of mosquitoes descended, they slapped and shouted. Darnell yelled "fuck" each time one got him. This brought a hefty man out of the next car. He had his wife and two teenage daughters with him and was not in the mood for it.

"What's wrong with you?" the man asked Darnell. "I got kids and my wife in that car. We can hear everything you're saying."

"These skeeters are bleedin' us dry."

"If you were fool enough to come here without mosquito spray you deserve what you're gettin'. Now shut up."

His demand infuriated Darnell, who shoved open the door and nutted the guy to get a head start. He jumped on the man and got in two solid licks before the wife and girls pounced on Darnell. One girl grabbed Darnell's earlobe and tried to yank it off. Their mother stomped on Darnell's crotch with her bare feet. The other daughter grabbed his hair and jerked. Darnell had an Elvis cut with too much Dapper Dan pomade. The girl's yanking caused black strands to separate and stick up like quills. He looked like an agitated porcupine. Ben tried to help the women pull Darnell off about the time men came from several rows of cars, along with an irritated drive-in manager.

Then came the cops, who arrested Darnell and Ben for assault. Fortunately the wife followed them to the police station and convinced officers that Ben had attempted to stop the fight rather than join it. Their dates had reefer on them given by Darnell in exchange for future favors. When they saw cops coming both skipped and hopped away on a gravel exit while trying to keep their heels on and not do a header in the rocks. After the mother's insistence a marshal handed Ben keys to the

Mercury and directed him to take it back to where it came from and never return to their jurisdiction.

The beautyshop and barbershop spread the word that Darnell and Ben were arrested for brawling with girls at a drive-in. Ben feared calling Pene when he heard the gossip, but she rang on Saturday afternoon with a brief message: "Come to the front gate on Sunday after church." He got in one word and a contraction before she hung up: "It wasn't…"

Pene's older brother Dennis walked out to the gate on Sunday. "Ben, I like you, and I'm sorry, but Pene comes first. She wanted to come out until Larry heard her say she'd rip off your arms and beat you to death with them. Larry has her cornered in a closet and won't let her out until you leave. So please go."

"Dennis, what they're sayin' didn't happen that way."

"Doesn't matter. Pene says you lied to her about Friday night and knew what would happen if you ever did. I'm sorry. But she's done with you for good. My sister is too bull-headed to ever change her mind. You should leave. If you need to talk to anyone in the family call me first. Please don't come here anymore. I don't want this to get ugly between me and you."

With no room to maneuver Ben surrendered. "I understand. Thanks for being straight with me. It's better to be slapped with the truth than kissed with a lie. So a Russian writer said."

From that moment on Pene avoided Ben. Difficult in a small town like Grinder's Switch. She wouldn't make eye contact. Talk to him. Go near him.

Richard hadn't heard about the melee and didn't care anyhow. Tuffy hired a lawyer for Darnell. After brief negotiations and cash changing hands Darnell came home, sort of. Tuffy beat him with a shovel while Bear and Connie held him down. Her chief complaint: He got Ben in this sordid mess and ruined his relationship with Pene. A nice girl from a good family. Tuffy threw Darnell out of the house and made Leon rent him a wrecked panel truck to sleep in. Leon complained mightily because Darnell wouldn't pay the first week's rent in advance.

Moving On

At the end of Ben's junior year Richard announced the higher education plan he had devised. A fraternity brother was vice chancellor at a liberal arts private college named Braynerd. It had about 600 students and was tucked away in a hamlet about an hour's drive from Chicago. Richard asked his friend to let Ben apply for a full scholarship there after undergoing an oral examination. Though an unusual proposal, the posh private school had a large endowment and numerous wealthy alumni. So it made its own rules. Appropriate faculty agreed.

Ben's satisfaction led him to tell Tuffy. Her eyes smiled.

When Tuffy called him for a sit-down at Dotty's café, Ben found Cutie and Connie in a booth with her. Cutie took over immediately. "We just want you to know how proud we are of you."

Tuffy intervened. "I don't know if you wanted me to tell anybody, but I got so excited I couldn't help myself. We're the only ones who know."

Wrong. The beautyshop and barbershop knew that an exclusive college had shown an interest in him. Perhaps his dad had bragged to a bartender. Connie's approval consisted of a quick nod. Ben became embarrassed by their praise and truncated the sit-down with a thin excuse to make his exit.

After accepting Braynerd's invitation Ben and his father drove off the morning of the interview and reached the college on time. Ben drove. Richard sipped enough vodka to drop a bison.

Richard's friend led Ben to an ornate meeting room where four professors waited around a ponderous wood table. Dark shelves stuffed with leather-bound volumes lined the room. Ben was supposed to be impressed. He was. The four wore conservative suits and ties. Cutie saved him from serious embarrassment by insisting that he go to Little Rock with her so she could buy him a nice suit, tie, and white shirt perfect for the occasion. The professors wore dead serious masks that signaled superior status and power. However, they didn't anticipate that Richard had prepared Ben for a graduate degree defense. They got bushwhacked. After brief introductions the questioners began. The first asked what Ben currently was reading.

"Pascal's *Pensées*, in French, sir." Their masks went blank. The oldest professor smiled and asked why, planning to expose this pretender. Ben talked about the French philosopher's theory of probability at enough length and depth to satisfy them. Their queries soon became more conversational in nature. Discussions ranged from Aristotle to Camus, and Ben held his ground. The youngest professor taught American history and asked a trap question about the order of each southern state's joining the Confederacy and why in that order.

Ben didn't know. "I can name the states, but not their entry dates. I'll have to look that one up and get back to you."

"Look it up?"

"Yes sir. Einstein advised we should never memorize anything that can be looked up."

"Are you pulling my leg?"

"No sir. Einstein said it. You can look it up." Ben knew he had prevailed but chose a humble mask. It worked.

Back in Grinder's Switch, Cutie pulled up in a cherry red Mercedes convertible with a palomino top and matching interior and found Ben shucking corn for Cletis. She had Bardot's pouty lips and tousled blonde hair. Ben said the first thing that came to mind. "Will you have my baby?"

"Can't, Sweetie. Never sleep with men I love."

"You look gorgeous."

"Thanks, a girl has to bloom wherever God plants her."

They sat on wooden steps side by side. "Nice ride."

"Yeah, Daggart went nuts when I bought it in Little Rock and called his banker to cover the check. Not my fault. I told him I was fixin' to buy a new car. I'm here to ask for a favor."

"Ask."

"I know I'm gettin' way ahead of myself, but here goes. I'm pregnant, and I want to name the boy Wesley because that's your middle name. I also want you to be his godfather when the time comes. Tuffy will help me raise him, along with Connie and Cletis. But you got to take over when he, and I know it's a boy, is ready for college and all that. Daggart is okay with anything as long as he only has to write the checks. Connie and Cletis believe it's a good idea. I don't care what the rest think."

"I accept. But I have no idea what a godfather does."

"Me neither. But we'll figure it out. Now you're goin' off to college. Just worry about that right now. The rest'll come in time." Cutie hugged him tight. "Sweetie, you'll never know how much I love having you in my life."

Ben hoped his high school graduation ceremony would bring at least a nod from Pene. It didn't. Tuffy herded her crew into the gym for the superintendent's cliché-ridden speech about leaving a safe harbor for unknown waters. Ben accepted tepid congratulations from his father and people he hardly knew. The celebration ended at Tuffy's with spiked cider, spicy pork rinds and concern about Cardinals pitching without Bob Gibson.

The day before he departed for college Ben met Tuffy at Dotty's. She asked for the sit-down. After they took a booth Tuffy began: "Richard called to tell me his people are coming to take him to what sounds like a rehab place in Nashville. He wants me to do something with the house."

"Does he want to sell it?"

"That's not gonna happen even if he does. It's your homeplace now. I asked Richard if he wants rent money, and he said he didn't care. I told him some day you might want to come back. He said to have the papers drawn up giving it to you, and he'd sign it over. I think he'll have to stay in Nashville from now on where his kin can see to him. I went inside the house. It's in bad shape."

"I know. What do you think we should do?"

"Here's something to think about. Cletis is gonna marry Donnalou. They can rent your house."

"That's what we'll do. But I'm not taking Cletis' money."

"Ben, you know Cletis won't do that. He'll call it freeloadin' and will never do it. You'll have to take a little rent money."

"No. I'll never take his money. You'll have to work that out with him."

"Or I can tell Connie you bowed up on me, and she's got to straighten you out. We'll see how long that takes."

"Hell no. Don't you dare sic her on me." After this stalemate a solution occurred. "Someone has to fix the house up. Let's cut a deal with Cletis where he does that instead of paying rent. That works for both of us. I'll pay for all the material."

"Connie is sharing a place with Cletis and Donnalou when they marry. She can help with the work."

"Okay. Please sell this to Cletis. I know you can."

"It gets better. Richard brought me a cashier's check for you, and it's for a whole lot of money he came into. I took it to Randall Miller at the bank. He put it in his safe until you can go see him and tend to the paperwork."

"How much is it?"

"A shitload. Now you go see Randall."

After these resolutions they ordered chocolate sundaes to celebrate. Then Ben asked a long-deferred question about Bear's health. "Bear is slipping bad. What caused his problems?"

"He got hurt tree-cuttin' years ago. The company wouldn't help until Judge Cody stepped in. Now they pay his medical bills and give us a monthly check."

Tuffy told Ben the long story. Preston Thompson, a vicious, corrupt man talked Bear into hiring his son Langston to represent Bear in a personal injury lawsuit. Langston graduated from a law school nobody ever heard of. Judge Cody was not in the mood for nonsense. Several witnesses swore Bear had come to work drunk that day and was crushed by a tree he cut down on himself. Still, Bear had a chance. Two arrogant young lawyers hired by the lumber company prepared their case too fast and easy. The jury pool swelled with kin and friends who wouldn't side against Bear no matter what. The two white-shoe lawyers, both city boys, showed up cocky. Hillbillies recognize condescension, even if they can't spell it.

After Judge Cody rushed through preliminaries Langston stood and asked to say a few words that would resolve the issue immediately. Both defense lawyers stood to object. But Judge Cody cut them off. They could talk after Langston finished.

Langston held up a copy of the U.S. Constitution and bellowed through his enraged lawyer mask: "Your Honor, this Constitution says nobody can discriminate against anybody else in this country. That includes drunkards. Bear had a few, but you can't hold that against him. I move you rule in his favor right now." The Ivy League shoes had not prepared for this constitutional argument and looked perplexed. After a brief comment to his Yale colleague the Harvard shoes stood. "Your Honor, we request an en camera conference in chambers."

"Figured you would after that. Come on." Judge Cody led Bear and the white shoes. Langston followed, pleased that someone might take his picture for the newspaper.

When they arrived the Judge issued a warning: "Whatever is said here stays here. If anyone repeats it he'll be found in contempt and thrown into a county jail cell where hungry rats are waitin'. Langston, I better not hear anymore bullshit out of you." He turned to the white shoes. "What do you gentlemen want?" The Harvard shoes stepped up: "Your Honor, what he said in court is ridiculous. We will immediately file for a mistrial and sanctions against opposing counsel."

"Thanks for sharing that. But I got my own problems. I don't need this aggravation. Maybe you boys didn't notice that all the jurors nodded in agreement while Langston was spouting his silly shit. Plus, that lumber company is owned by a family of thieves who've been stealing money from these folks since the war. Pick any war you want. You can't win this one."

The Harvard shoes: "Perhaps we should seek a change of venue."

"Perhaps you should. But if you do, count on their kin burning down the mill while you're doing it. They'll not have rich thieves denying Bear and Tuffy a little money for eats and aspirin. Langston, how much do Bear and Tuffy need each month to get by?"

"Five thousand should do."

Judge Cody threw an empty coffee mug on his desk at Langston, who barely ducked in time. The white shoes shuffled backwards. "They'll get a thousand and medical expenses. These gentlemen will sort that out. If not, the fire marshal will inspect that mill every day. I know it's a death trap. It'll stay shut down for a few years until it passes muster with every acronym in government. Now all of you gentlemen put an end to this nonsense."

"How much will I get paid for my legal services," Langston said.

"Not a damn thing. Ask daddy to increase your allowance."

"The judge saved us," Tuffy said, ending the story. "Bear don't talk about that or much else anymore. It's hard to watch a big, squared-up man like him go inside himself and never come out. Bear lets me shampoo his hair when nobody is around. He likes that a lot. That's about all we got left now." She stared hard. "Ben, you get out of this place, even if you got to crawl out on bleedin' knees."

First Things First

The campus had large, four-story brick buildings filled with comfortable apartments fit for four students. These old structures formed a horseshoe and had a grass-filled park between them. Picnic tables and wood lawn chairs were scattered on the grass so students could gather and discuss issues currently in vogue on campuses. The scene offered sunlight dialogues between privileged kids wearing masks of intellectual and moral superiority. The opening of this horseshoe led to flat white buildings with classrooms, administrative offices, faculty spaces and a cafeteria. The gym had a swimming pool and space for gawkers to check flesh tones. Faculty members who strolled through with recon eyes made clear that such physical displays didn't interest them. They were shortcutting to reach a Malcolm X seminar.

As Ben lugged two suitcases into the building where he would stay, a student volunteer led him to an apartment on the third floor. He saw one roommate, casually dressed and clean cut, sitting at a desk. He stood and shook Ben's hand. "Hello. I'm Nelson Steadman."

"Pleased to meet you Nelson. Ben Hart."

"Our two roommates are Durkey and Rod, who are in the bathroom smoking pot with the air filter on high speed. I hope you don't mind me asking if you're normal."

"Compared to them I'm normal. Don't use drugs and don't want to be around anyone who does. So first thing, I'll tell them our new drug-free policy. I expect you to back me."

"I will. Where are you from?"

"I'm an Ozark hillbilly. I'm on a full scholarship and cannot get cuffed and perp-walked out of here with two junkies in a sweep."

"I can't either. I'm preparing for an investment banking career with my father's Chicago firm. I'm already on edge. He graduated magna cum laude from here, and I'm not that smart. Glad to have you."

"Wait until you hear what I say to Cheech and Chong."

"Don't worry. I'll have your back."

As if cued, Rod and Durkey came out of the bathroom riding a cloud of smoke. They walked up and shook Ben's hand. He immediately made Durkey for a tweaker and side-dealer. His long dirty hair and blotched skin repelled Ben. Rod had blond hair, a lifter's body, and wore Brooks Brothers chinos and Italian loafers without socks. Both reeked of arrogance and privilege in addition to reefer. Some of that disappeared when Ben spoke. "Before I assign your house-keeping chores I have a brief message. Both of you get any illegal drugs out of here immediately. If not, I'll arrange to have my junkie cousin tip off narcotics cops for some perks at the county jail, his current home. He will snitch you out for a carton of Camels, and you can take turns getting sodomized by

violent men with bad breath. Don't ever keep drugs here. I'll toss your stuff occasionally to look for stash and call Darnell to drop the dime if I find any. At this point you might be thinking a better solution would be for you to run me off. But that ain't gonna happen. If you try I'll throw Durkey out that window. Rod, you're big and buff so I may wait until you doze off and use that fireplace iron to beat you in the head until blood runs out. You can tell cops the beat-down came because you wouldn't stop selling narcotics to these college kids. Let me know how that plays at your daddy's country club."

Nelson interrupted. "I should add that my family's attorneys, all of them, will be representing Ben in these matters. Since I am privy to this conversation and your illegal drug use in the apartment I will be required to testify against you."

Durkey and Rod departed immediately to review options.

"Never allow me to make you angry," Nelson said.

"That wasn't me talking. It was my cousins and hillbilly thugs."

"Where is your family from exactly?"

"We are exactly scattered throughout the hills, running wild with razorbacks and rattlers."

Durkey and Rod decided to play by Ben's rules, or pretend to. Durkey rarely came around. Rod found comfort and shelter with attractive co-eds. Nelson and Ben partnered up and scouted the campus for desirable females. Nelson described the co-eds as too anguished about America's huddled masses to have an orgasm. During a search inside the library's rotunda Ben saw several young women handing out fliers. A pretty brunette named Willow with long hair pulled back in a ponytail approached. "Will you join us?" she asked.

"For what?"

"We are raising funds and soliciting volunteers to help with our goal of saving life in the Orinoco Basin. We plan to lead a group of students down there to protest the government's failure to respect and protect animal and plant life."

"I may be too busy for the trip, but I'll give you all my money." He pulled out two dollars and handed them to her. "Here, this is my life savings."

Willow looked up, unable to form an appropriate response, so he continued. "Now I no longer have money for supper. That means you will have to buy me what may be the only meal I get today."

She smiled. "I have worked here for a week and heard every pick-up line there is, or so I thought. What do you expect me to buy you?"

"A greasy cheeseburger and fries."

"How about the Whole Earth Café."

"No. I don't want a tofu burger and fruit."

"Cheeseburgers are not good for you."

"Willow, nothing I do is good for me. Are you going to provide nourishment or not?"

"My shift ends in 30 minutes. Come back then. We'll eat in the cafeteria."

"They serve rabbit food."

"I know. But the room is well lit and full of witnesses."

Ben smiled. "You think I may be a serial killer?"

"I'm not sure yet."

During her break he searched the library for anything on the basin and found its location in South America.

After they sat down Willow said, "When I mentioned Orinoco did you know its location?"

"Not then. But I do now. And I ain't going with you. Snakes down there are big enough to swallow a Peterbilt. You people are nuts."

They spent a pleasant hour or so talking about culture and classes. "I want to see you again," he said.

"I will give you my phone number, but no address. Call me about next weekend. One problem with you is I will have to do research after every cheeseburger."

"Why?"

"First, to find out what a Peterbilt is. Before I look, is it something obscene?"

"No. You need to hang out at truck stops. Men there are more worldly than college boys. They like their outlaw life and don't care what anyone thinks about it. In that respect they are my extended family."

"No thanks. I can't believe a thing you say."

Willow later decided, wisely, that an affair with Ben would be disastrous. During her avocado salad, side of chickpeas and cup of herbal tea Willow explained in excruciating detail how she reached this decision. He listened with a sensitive mask and asked for the check.

By end of his first week Ben had attended the first session of all his classes and projected how little he could do to succeed: Freshman Composition, French One, Geography, American History, Philosophy. When an assistant professor returned their first essays Ben had an A on the cover. Glancing around he saw expressions ranging from strained to unhinged. A sexy blonde near him looked at Ben's bluebook and blushed.

After critical commentary from their instructor the class began to file out past him at the door. The LA blonde caught Ben. "Hi. I'm Kelly, and I need your help." Her smile highlighted creamy cheeks and perfect white teeth. After sweeping a strand of lovely hair away from her big blue eyes she issued her first command. "I'll talk to you in the hall." He stared at her movements in tight white shorts and a perky polo then turned toward Delph, the teacher.

Delph: "I know. God help you." Ben sensed that Kelly would be a mistake worth making so he did. But after weeks maneuvering him to do all her work for an occasional blow job he quit. This suited Nelson, who needed his help more than she did.

Ben and Delph frequently had coffee after Ben's first essays. Delph knew immediately that intellectually Ben could lift anything put in front of him. They sometimes differed on literary merits of writers but knew one could make sound arguments either way. When Ben mentioned his tutorial resignation Delph said, "I'm pleased someone learned something useful in my class. Anything else going on?"

"No. I'm between rare sexual exploits. How about you?"

"You are the first to know that after this term I will be moving on. I have taken an opening at Michigan. It is tenure track and may eventually make my career financially sustainable."

"I'll miss you. They are fortunate to get you. I mean it. Congratulations."

"Thank you. I appreciate that. However, since I am still your instructor I must deliver a lecture I should have given long ago. You are not showing me what is under the hood of that fast car you drive. You always gravitate toward the Brits. At first I thought it was because you recognize that their best are better than our best. But I have come to believe you are crossing an ocean to stay far away and difficult to follow. I am not asking to hear your confession because I'm Methodist. However, I propose that you trust me. Don't hide behind cleverness and Ezra's empty space. Do me an essay on Dreiser's *American Tragedy*. Tell me about that young man hiding so much.

Take me where that goes. Maybe I'll discover what is generating all your horsepower."

Ben's next date came about after he read aloud in class his essay on Rousseau. An attractive art major talked him into going with her to a Chicago Art Institute exhibition. He did okay until they stood in front of a celebrated work consisting of steel pipes connected to form an arcane configuration. Bryana: "What do you think it means?"

Ben: "Two things. First, it means the artist owns a huge Crescent wrench. Second, it means Warhol is right when he says art is what you can get away with."

The ride back to campus was awkward.

Normally a philosophy class would never command Ben's attention. But one did. An arrogant student chose to duel in class with an elderly Jewish professor. The debate centered on Sartre's *Being and Nothingness*. Ben started the book but didn't finish. At first he welcomed existentialism into his universe. A world without God. Man determines his morals. But when Sartre expanded his ideas Ben couldn't fully follow the

French intellectual's complex philosophical reasoning. Ben chose not to fake it. The presumptuous philosophy major couldn't follow it either but tried to fake it. Verbal thrusts and parries between this wise man and a pretender entertained Ben. The professor patiently, politely, shredded the student's persona. The event supported one of Connie's guiding principles: If you don't know what you're talking about, then shut the fuck up.

Connie called. Wesley was born with all his toes and fingers. Cutie would call whenever. Goodbye.

Ben's next social engagement became treacherous. Nelson's sister Laura wanted her brother to bring a friend and take her, along with her friend Serena, to a birthday dinner at an expensive Chicago restaurant. Nelson told his sister that he roomed with an "intellectual phenom," and Laura wanted to meet him.

"Which one is my date?"

"Serena," Nelson replied, but something in his tone lit Ben's red light.

"Why am I matched with her?"

"Because Serena gets on my nerves."

"Why."

"She dresses like that woman in *The Adams Family* and chain smokes."

"I'm out."

"Please go because I told Laura you would since it's her birthday celebration. Plus, I'll buy you the Elmore James and Bill Evans vinyl you can't afford."

"Okay, but you tell Serena she will not light up at our table."

Nelson drove them downtown. Laura and Serena took a cab. When Laura got out Ben saw a nicely turned out, pretty young woman in a tight black designer dress. Her jewelry probably cost more than a John Deere tractor. Serena looked impeccably weird in a tight black jumpsuit. Coal black hair in a crewcut. Way too much dark makeup. Ben broke the black ice walking in: "You will not smoke at our table."

"No shit," Serena said.

After they sat down Nelson led the conversation down obscure paths: Miles Davis fusion. New Wave French auteurs. Nelson didn't know a damn thing about any of this until after his artistic deep dive the previous week. His strategy purposely abbreviated their dining experience. Ben remained bored until Laura's bare foot rubbed his thigh beneath the table. Serena appeared lost in her murky cranial cavity after two dry martinis.

After their torte Laura put an arm inside Ben's for an escort out. When far behind Nelson and Serena: "You didn't say much, Ben. Was something on your mind?"

"Look. We both know you're not a slut. So stop winding me up. I'm here out of respect for your brother. You should be ashamed." Laura walked out without responding.

Ben had read much of the material assigned in classes while under his father's tutelage and had endured Richard's merciless examinations. During melancholy moments he sometimes recalled visions of Pene in cut-off jeans and a Razorback t-shirt walking among the cattle she adored. Pene petted them and whispered in their ears about how much she loved them. Sweet moments. Probably the best in his life. Ben mourned their passing every time memories made them vivid.

Some Grinder's Switch recollections were vastly different. In an American History class Ben studied fallout after Pickett ordered his Virginians to make their disastrous July 3 charge across that Gettysburg meadow. The debacle brought to mind a confrontation between Uncle Penrod Doss and Judge Cody. Penrod passed the crazy test with Confederate Colors flying. He claimed to have been named after a heroic Rebel army officer named Doss who died in battle. But the barbershop said that Doss had been shot by his own men for siphoning off their food rations to sell on the black market.

Penrod dressed in a Confederate officer uniform. Kept his black hair straight and oiled. Beard slicked down with bear grease. Tried to herd his hogs in military rows with a swagger stick. His holiday hog march didn't happen because Judge Cody wouldn't let them in the Christmas parade. The judge stopped Penrod from disgorging his hogs from a bob truck. Judge Cody: "Those pigs are not going to shit all over Main Street today. I sent for Lulu to bring your boys and carry you home. Don't you ever come back here with those pigs or the American Legion will host a free pork barbecue."

Cutie called late at night: "Ben?"

"Cutie. Are you okay?"

"Yeah. You got time to talk or is somebody there."

"Only Pynchon with his *Gravity's Rainbow*. I'm so sick of this book. Is Wesley okay?"

"Doin' great. Sometimes he gets on Daggart's nerves. Makes my day. Actually, that's not fair. I called because Daggart is supposed to be doing something nice for him. But we got to watch out."

"What."

"He is settin' up a large trust fund for Wesley with you and me in charge. I couldn't figure out what he might be up to until I talked to Connie. She heard Daggart was asking around about you and learned you're super smart and special. He knows the two of us call the shots about Wesley. His other son Pence is a junkie and too stupid to be the village idiot. Daggart wants our attention. My Little

Rock shyster looked at the paperwork and says it's clean. But I won't consider it till you say okay. I'm sorry, Sweetie, but you're all I got."

"Cutie, I'll help. But I don't know when I can come down there. Can you send the paperwork up here?"

"I'll do whatever it takes 'cause I'm in way over my head."

The day Cutie came they had lunch, reviewed the paperwork and made plans. When they walked out of the cafeteria Rod was by the front door among a handful of worshipful girls. When he approached, Cutie made him right away. Rod held out his hand to her and slipped on his Number One smile. Cutie struck without coiling. "Honey, you do have a pretty smile, but you need to save it for these young ladies. They might believe the bullshit that goes with it. I won't." Rod's mask fell, revealing astonishment in lavender shades. After Rod sulked away Ben said, "I'm impressed."

"Sweetie, that's just a slow curve. You should see my heat."

Ben heard Rod was training his fraternity puppets to dominate desirable, difficult-to-win women. Rod shared lurid descriptions of a recent conquest called Laura. Nelson's Laura heard about this from a friend at the college and called Ben. "Can I see you?"

"When?"

"Now. I'm at a phone booth outside the library."

"I'll be right there." When Ben arrived Laura looked out the car window but couldn't maintain eye contact.

Ben got in: "Do you want to talk, or is it too raw?"

"Do you know what Rod has done?"

"I heard."

"What has he said about me?"

"Don't know and don't want to know. Does Nelson know?"

"I don't think so. He is still at the lake house and probably doesn't know about it."

Laura told her story between sniffles: "I was here visiting a friend and ran into Rod at the pool. He talked me into going to a motel room with him to smoke a joint. But it was a lot stronger than I thought. There must have been something in a vodka shot he gave me first. Rod got me high and made me strip and do some awful stuff with him. Really awful. My life is over."

"No, not over, just harder. Does your family know?"

"My sister Diane knows something is wrong, but not what happened."

"I'll take you to my favorite truck stop for coffee. We'll come up with a cover story for your distress and a plan to handle Rod. Get your head around this before you talk to anyone else. I'll handle Rod. I'll hurt him bad."

Ben's meeting the next night with Rod got tetchy fast. "First item: I got an anonymous call from a guy who says you got to be gone by sunrise. Said if that doesn't happen the following will. He'll tip off the college newspaper that you assaulted and raped a woman. He'll provide your name and the motel where it happened. Mr.

Anonymous knows all the details necessary to make the story stick with the cops. They'll be way up your ass in a hurry. He also said if you ever contact or go near the woman the price goes up. There is no statute of limitations on personal destruction. Make sure you leave campus on time or the alarm goes off."

Rod attempted to maintain a threatening mask, but it couldn't cover the fear. "You fucking asshole. You're a white trash hick, and I know what you're doing. I'll kill you for it."

"Sorry you feel that way Rod. I'm only the messenger."

"I'm coming after you. Count on it."

When the deadline arrived Rod drove away. Laura called Ben that afternoon to say thanks and that she and Nelson were transferring to Northwestern. Nelson asked her to tell Ben goodbye.

A New Plan

Year One ended with excellent grades and a new plan. Ben decided to graduate in three years. Frequent yawns convinced him. Before summer classes Ben returned to the hills for iced tea and sparkling conversation. He visited Tuffy and Bear first. Her hip hurt. Bear dozed. Nothing new there. Ben stopped at the hog barn and found Cletis scattering corn in a wood trough. He saw Ben pick up a sack of corn to help. "I'm not paying you for that."

"I know. You're too tight."

They half-hugged. "Tuffy told me you and Connie are now co-in-charge. How's that working out for you?"

"When I tell her to shut up she quiets down for about sixty seconds. About as long as her marriage lasted."

"I know she married briefly. What happened?"

"Tommy farms with his family a few hills west of here. He courted her for two or three months and promised to stop drinking. The men in that family are power drinkers and hard on their women. We didn't think he was stupid enough to try anything with Connie, but he was. He roughed her up one night. After he went to sleep Connie crawled on top of him with a skinnin' knife and held it tight against his throat. That woke him up. She told Tommy if she sliced through an artery he'd not last two minutes.

"Connie told him she'd ask Judge Cody in the morning to get her a divorce and Tommy better go along. Just so he'd remember to never come near her again she carved a shallow red ring around his throat.   He ran off

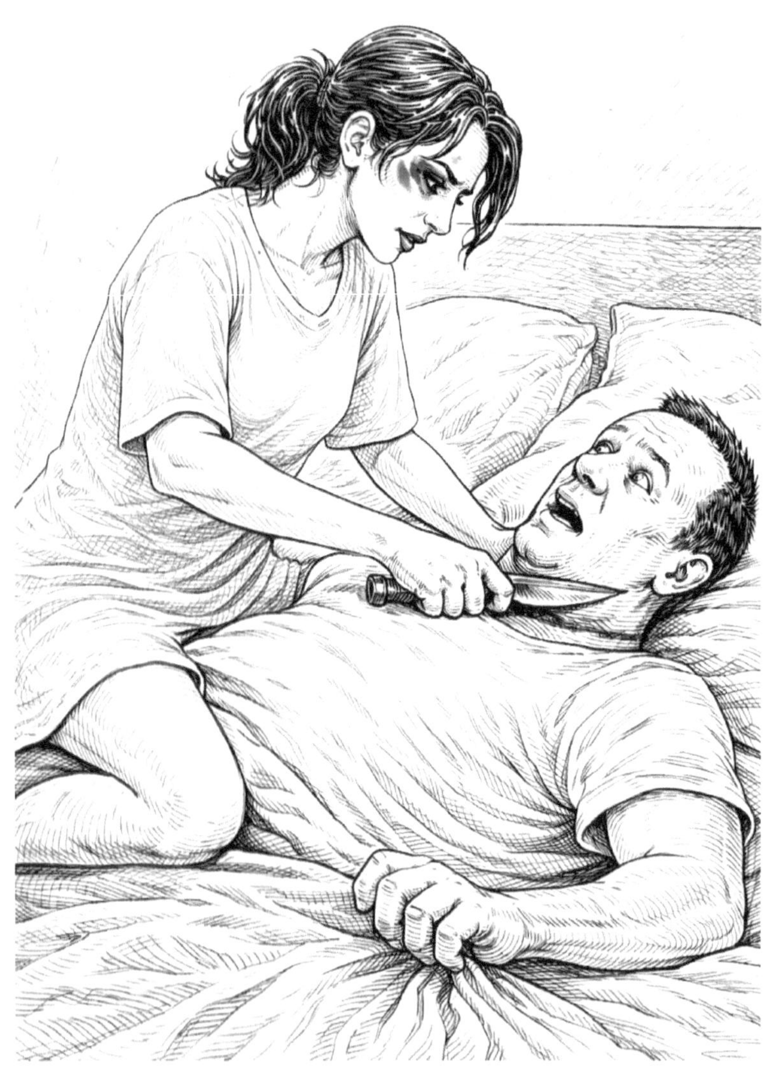

as soon as she finished. Nobody wanted to date her after that."

Darnell was in the county jail again. Cletis told Ben to go see him, even if he didn't want to. He was kin. When Ben walked into the visitor area Darnell began his con. "Boy, you're lookin' real good and educated. Look here. I'm workin' on a GRE. Gonna go to college when I get out on parole. Boy in here has a cousin that works at a fancy college out west. He can get me in, but it's gonna cost. I got to get cash fast."

"What college are you talking about?"

"He won't give me the name till I give him the money."

"Can't help you with the money."

"Ask Cutie to loan you some. After she gives you the money it's yours to do what you want. You loan it to me, and I'll pay you back every month with interest till we're slick. You pay her back and pocket the interest. Whatta deal, huh?"

Ben stood. "Before I go to Cutie you'll need a detailed budget. Call when it's ready." Darnell's wide eyes watched that curtain come down.

Leon also got bad news. Ella, his latest fiancée, dumped him after finding out Leon kept up a lap dancer for sleepovers in Memphis. Tuffy was pissed. Bear was pissed. The priest that counselled them was pissed. Her family had demanded that he join their church before the marriage. The only reason Leon proposed was to get near her family money. Papa had congestive heart disease and wasn't supposed to live much longer. But he lived long enough to save his daughter from Leon.

After returning for summer school Ben met his new academic mentor. Professor Karl Raynor assigned his southern fiction class an essay on *The Bear*. Ben considered it an opportunity to mimic Faulkner's idiosyncratic prose. He used serpentine sentences implausibly tied together by clauses. Invented words. Strange syntax shifts. Made-up punctuation. When Raynor returned his bluebook Ben saw an A on the front page and this note: "I get it, but if you ever pull this stunt again I will assign you a long paper on *Finnegans Wake* and demand several re-writes. The gauntlet has been thrown and welcome back to the land of a thousand blind monkeys."

Weeks later Tuffy called to say Bear died in his sleep of an aneurysm. After arriving in Grinder's Switch for the service Ben stored his gear at his rent house. Cletis, Donnalou and Connie insisted. They had made many improvements, and Ben paid Connie after a tour.

She warned Ben yet again: "Don't ever let Darnell know Richard gave you a lot of money. You have no idea how dangerous Darnell is now along with his runnin' buddies. They're a bad lot and will do anything for money. I trained you for trouble, but you can't handle their kind. I'm serious."

"Connie, you worry too much."

"Ben, your problem is you don't know how much you don't know. Brains aren't enough against people like them. There are no rules. Now pay attention to everything I said." She gave him a half-hug and walked off. Ben filed her info.

Tuffy kept the funeral crowd sparse after making it clear to everyone it was family only. When Ben arrived

Cutie made everyone slide down the pew so she could put Wesley between them. Family entrances gave Ben close looks in quiet time. Tuffy came in using a cane, led by Connie. Donnalou kept pace with a solemn Cletis while carrying their little boy.

Cutie looked conservatively sexy. Darnell looked predictably intoxicated. Leon looked furious. He had traded the funeral home director a used Ford station wagon for an expensive casket. However, the director stopped him outside the chapel door and complained that the Ford had a leaky radiator and ran hot all the time. He demanded boot for the casket. Or after Bear's funeral his body would be dumped in a hole. Leon had to peel off some hundreds from his gangster roll to resolve their dispute before services commenced

After returning to campus Ben heard another new plan. Raynor asked him to become his assistant and help with research, grade papers, and lecture when Raynor worked in a lay-up with a female student. Ben took the deal and got a small private room on campus. This arrangement continued into Year Two. Well into that year he sat at his kitchen table grading papers when a student knocked. "What," Ben yelled. The knocker yelled back: "A woman named Laura is downstairs asking for you."

Ben stopped red lining a student's mediocre essay on Eliot and hustled downstairs.

When he saw her smiling they full-hugged. Laura stood beside her sister Diane and made a grand introduction. "Diane, this is Ben, my white knight."

He shook hands with Diane and turned to Laura. "Girl, you be lookin' mighty fine, as my cousin Darnell would say when he's out on bail and horny."

Both women laughed. Laura: "After having a few beers with Nelson he tells me Doss stories. They are hilarious."

"And regrettably they are too close to true. Is Nelson here? I'd like to see him."

"Waiting in the cafeteria. Nelson wanted us to have some personal time first." Diane exited before Laura continued. "He has been so sweet, Ben. He knows all of it."

Ben sensed she needed to talk so they sat on a bench. The warm sunlight put a glow on Laura's lovely complexion, but she seemed embarrassed. "Don't ever look back, Laura. Nietzsche got it wrong. It doesn't make you stronger. But over time you learn how best to deploy the pain."

"One of the reasons I wanted to talk to you is to apologize for the way I acted at Charlie Trotter's restaurant the first time we met. I'm still mortified."

"You shouldn't be. It helped take my mind off Serena. And let's skip the part where we apologize for all the stupid shit we've done in our lives because my list is much longer than yours. What else is on your mind?"

"Well, top of the list is I got married to an older guy I knew from years ago. Clark is a good man. I began to see him after I stopped crying all the time and decided to get on with it. He is an architect. I knew it was much too soon, but I was afraid nobody else would want me. I haven't told Clark my story. Do you think I should?"

"You got to own that one alone. But be one hundred percent certain before you do. No doubts about the turnout."

"The hitch is I love Clark, but I'm not truly in love with him, if you understand the difference."

"I do."

As Laura revealed the pain from her past, Ben's view of Rod plunged from animus to intense hatred. Ben believed that what Laura endured had been experienced by many women Rod tortured. Laura talked for a while, uncovered all the scars and closed with an apology: "I'm sorry. But I needed to talk to you because we share that history. I must look awful."

"No you don't. I see a bright, classy, beautiful lady. Clark is lucky you said yes. Now stay in your lane. You're going the right direction." They hugged again, and their tight grip made both feel stronger than they were.

Ben found Nelson waiting, and they shook hands. "Laura is well on her way to the other side," Ben said.

"I know, thanks to you. However, this story has a worrisome follow-up about you."

"How so."

"As soon as Laura told me the story I began plans for Rod's remaining days on Earth. My personal attorney and long-time close friend uses an independent group of investigators for special problems. They're mostly ex-cops. One of their out-sourced associates is a man named Lee who scorches the earth when necessary. My friend called Lee and put him in touch with me. He is ex-military and exceptionally able. We agreed on his fee, and Lee developed a strategy to ruin Rod's life. Lee planted leaks about rape and kidnapping with people who mattered. Maybe I should feel bad about this, but I don't, not after what he did to Laura. To finance his entitled life, Rod partnered with Durkey to sell drugs to high-end buyers. Apparently his parents cut Rod off after bad news reached town. While investigating Rod, Lee found out he has a bad heroin habit. I'm compressing this into bullet points because Lee wants to wall you off from a lot of it. Lee learned that Rod is consumed by hatred and may become a problem for Laura and you. I retain Lee to watch and consult when appropriate. Ben, Lee has enormous resources. I'm sure he can handle anything anywhere. All he plans to do now is watch and listen. Lee will let me know if he needs to step in.

"Lee squeezed Durkey and found out Rod knows how to find you in the hills. Lee convinced Durkey that if something bad happens to you or Laura he'll be held responsible and die slow. Durkey is now Lee's informant."

"I visit Grinder's Switch occasionally to check on my aunt's health." Ben said. "If Rod shows up there my kin will take care of it."

"Don't forget that Laura is at risk too. Please let Lee handle it for both of you. I'm getting the check."

"Okay. You got it."

"May I ask a personal question?"

"Ask."

"Long ago you said something when we were having lunch at the cafeteria that stuck with me. You said that smiley masks come off when barbarians breach the wall. Is that where I am now? I'm asking because I have been doing things I would never have done had Rod not crushed Laura. I won't stop until he is destroyed."

"Nelson, keep in mind that my mask theories are personal. I don't recommend them to others because of what they do to you. My cynicism is second only to Diogenes. Find your own way to see through all the lies and deceit around you."

The wait for Rod took about a year. Durkey told Lee when Rod decided to get even with the guy who ruined his life. Lee contacted Ben, who referred him to Connie. Rod drove into Grinder's Switch in a rental and headed to Ben's house where he expected to find Ben alone thanks to a false lead. Instead, Rod found Connie in a rocking chair with a police special under the blanket in her lap. She appeared decrepit. Rod knocked on the door. Connie yelled "Come in." He did, holding a pistol behind his back. "Is Ben here?"

"No, but he'll be right back. Have a seat."

"Okay, I'm a college friend so I'll wait." Completely misjudging the situation, Rod slipped the gun beneath his belt and sat down.

Connie had counted on this. She raised her .38 and pulled back the hammer. Rod froze. "Smiley, you look godawful. Cutie said you had a great smile and cut a nice figure. Now look at you. You always were a piece of shit, now you look like one."

"Who are you?"

"I'm payback for all the women you've hurt, every one of 'em."

Ben walked in from the kitchen and startled Rod. "What is this?" Rod gasped.

"It's what preachers around here call the end of days," Ben replied as he walked to Connie and took the pistol.

Ben turned toward Rod, who pulled out his gun. That made it easy. Ben shot him in the head before Rod could aim.

Lee rushed in: "Let's get him in that abandoned mine shaft you showed me. Connie and I will scrub here when we get back."

"It was self-defense. Any judge will agree," Ben said.

"We ain't goin' to court," Connie said. "That's just a place lawyers go to lie for money. This maggot meat is going in a deep hole. You're not at fault for any of this. So get past it fast. Connie shot Rod in the chest for a second opinion and kept the gun for disposal.

They bought sandwiches and sodas on their return. After an extensive forensic scrub down, Lee gave them background between bites. Durkey told Lee about Rod's planned trip to Grinder's Switch. Lee and Connie agreed on the plan after she convinced Lee she would kill Rod if Ben wouldn't. Her kin. Her call. Lee got it.

Mice and Markers

Ben made a scene in film class. Professor Filander became incensed by his argument that Ingmar Bergman was a con artist. Though "technically proficient," said Ben, the Swedish director claimed to reveal profound insight in his films. "Nonsense." Bergman was a pretentious bore. Ben recommended the class skip Bergman and instead run Doris Day movies in search of BCE symbolism.

After these and other high art heresies Filander called Raynor, which led to a sit-down with Ben. "What the hell are you doing to Filander. He's foaming at the mouth."

"Filander thinks he's James Agee, and he ain't."

"He also thinks he's Edmund Wilson, and he ain't," Raynor said. "So let us move on to more important matters. I assume you plan to graduate with no prospects whatsoever. You may not want it, but I can get you an associate professor position here. You will have a meager salary until you get something better. But you will have to shut up and smile when appropriate. I will help you get an MA and more if you work for me during the slog. However, I will not waste my time and markers with faculty unless you play their game with a straight face. So, my friend, which turn at the fork?"

"How did you get all these markers?"

"Many men have the same bad habits I do, and I know about them."

"Well, men are less monogamous than mice."

"How do you know that?"

"A Swiss study. What else they got to do there. I accept your offer because I don't want to teach freshman English at Crazy Town High School. Thanks for your help, yet again. I'm kinda bad at saying thanks, but thanks."

A few days after this conversation Connie called to say that Darnell died in a fiery car crash while chased by Oklahoma troopers. He and the meth he was hauling burned up. Tuffy stuffed his black bones in a bucket and buried them in a hole near Bear's grave. However, feral dogs dug them up for take-out.

Ben's forced march further into academia began with an essay for Filander on dangers of authoritarianism based on Nurse Ratched in *One Flew Over the Cuckoo's Nest*. Filander liked it a lot and others that followed, particularly those excoriating American capitalism. From that point on Ben wore an intellectual mask. Each day he filled anxious young minds with academic nonsense only a French intellectual could believe. His days passed too quickly to be seized. This went on for a bunch of years, and Cutie shifted more of Wesley's future to his godfather. They began to size up each other at Dotty's during occasional cheeseburgers, shakes and discussions about art. Ben prepared reading lists for their phoners. Wesley was real smart and quick. Grinder's Switch was not. When Wesley was to graduate from the eighth grade Ben called Cutie for a sit-down.

"He can't stay here any longer. The school and culture are harmful to someone with his potential. He's wasting valuable time. What I propose will throw you into an extended crying jag and clinical depression, but you asked me to take charge. Do you still want me to do that?"

Cutie's chin sank to her chest. "I knew this day was comin'. I knew it. Are you gonna take him away from me?"

"Not from you. From this place."

"Goddamn you, Ben. Goddamn you. One of the reasons I picked you was I knew you were hard enough inside to do what it would take. I'm not."

"Cutie, we don't have to do this my way."

"Sweetie, he's your boy too. What would you have for your boy?"

"Bradley White is a former graduate student of mine and headmaster at a private Catholic prep school in Chicago. It's a classical education in the finest sense. They have a dormitory closely monitored with advisors and tutors. You don't have to be Catholic to attend. Wesley can go to a required weekly mass to enjoy the inspiring Bach and ignore the Catholic crap. I'm about an hour away, and Chicago is rich in artistic and cultural opportunities. The school is popular with prominent families and smart kids. We want him around people like that for future networking."

"You think they'll let him in?"

"He's already in if he wants the spot. I'll set up an appointment with the master for a visit."

Cutie wore a conservative outfit Ben selected and remained mostly silent during Wesley's interview. Wesley had an edge, however: First, Ben's tutorials, which included Greek and Latin philosophers as well as Biblical history. Second, Cutie's "it" smile, which made her irresistible.

Bradley ended the session by announcing he was looking forward to having Wesley in his classes.

Cutie closed the deal. "Bradley, please forgive my ignorance, but all this is new to me. Is there a problem if I come visit Wesley sometimes if he's not too busy. I'll write for permission if I need to."

"No. Absolutely not. You just call me when you want to come. I'll give you my personal number. I'm looking forward to it."

Ben suppressed his amusement, but not his thought that this master was about to be home-schooled by a real master. Wesley would be in good hands. Ben could move on to other matters.

Madmen and Politicians

Being a full professor had its advantages: More money. Private pursuits while claiming to do research. Opportunities for outrageous lectures. All these benefits, and he couldn't be fired or arrested for what he said in class. Ben teed up caustic commentary: Why Byron's preference for young Italian boys at sleepovers. Opportunities for action-packed gunfights in Chekov's plays. Nasty sexual repartee in page-turners by Henry James. His lectures won high marks on student evaluations. Unfortunately they unleashed cultural provocateurs. This went on for years. Then Dean Foster showed up at Ben's office door. Several faculty members came up with the idea of beginning Ezra Pound seminars focused on *The Cantos*. Ben considered this long epic the Mount Everest of English literature. He climbed but never conquered. Even Pound called parts of it unfathomable.

The department decided Ben would teach *The Cantos* every other semester and dedicate other time to research. Born in Idaho, but a European wanderer, the poet was a cantankerous genius. Authorities charged him with treason for wartime radio broadcasts from Europe supporting axis fascism. A U. S. court found him mentally unfit for trial and put Pound in an insane asylum from 1946 to 1958. It took Hemingway and other literary superstars to help get him released.

Ben should begin preparations immediately, Foster said, since he would no longer be teaching other literature classes. However, *The Cantos* made his exile acceptable.

Ben needed a researcher to help and already had one in bed with him. Sophia, an Italian professor, had degrees from the Sorbonne in medieval literature.

Esoteric stuff, but helpful background for *The Cantos*. She also taught at Braynerd. Sophia enjoyed his rakish persona. He liked her accent so they shared her bed. Sophia's culinary skills explained her robust figure and his expanding waistline. They weighed weekly, sighed deeply and cursed the stars.

She joined the Pound project after Ben talked Foster into giving her a research stipend. Now he could do research in bed with a naked woman who made excellent tiramisu. Things were looking up.

Until Ben got a call from Leon asking for a sit-down. He wouldn't talk about it on the phone so they met in the college cafeteria. Leon said Langston had announced his candidacy for the U. S. House of Representatives. At first this didn't scare Ben as much as it should have since he considered Langston a losing bet.

Prematurely. Leon had become Langston's campaign manager. As Leon told the story Ben began to reassess Langston's chances. Lobbyists representing farm supply retailers, implement dealers and timber companies trailed Leon in the manner of carpenter ants. Sharpers brought checks from murky political action committees. This delighted Langston's father, Preston. He had become filthy rich and evil running a crime empire that included drug smuggling and selling. Preston owned a chain of liquor stores and honkytonks throughout the region. Most sold anything to anyone with cash. Preston pocketed the campaign contributions and learned politicians could strike gold while giving someone else the shaft.

But Langston's wife, Louella, became a problem. All the smiling at political functions made her jaws sore. Wearing a corset caused a rash on rollover fat. Strong pain pills made her wobbly.

It became embarrassing so Leon intervened. "We got to do something about Louella."

"Make her stay home," Preston said

"Can't do that. The other side might start rumors Langston is queer. That Louella found his butt boy in a closet. All our people hate homos." So Leon had Louella say hello to the crowd briefly before locking her in his car trunk during campaign events.

Leon developed an effective campaign strategy based on his car-lot principles. Never let suckers look under the hood. Test drive the vehicle. Rev-up the engine beyond short bursts. Keep it waxed in sunlight all day long. He managed Langston's campaign that way. Leon bribed a hospital orderly for names and addresses of seriously ill children and hired an unemployed TV cameraman to go with Leon and Langston to the child's home. Langston held the sick kid in his arms and bellowed toward the camera: "Here's why I'm running for Congress. To help our children and folks who deserve better." Langston closed by swearing he was deeply committed to a free press, and voters could count on him for complete transparency.

When sympathetic images of Langston and the kids reached TV screens, campaign center telephones reverberated in kind. Kin working for a cut answered and told callers where to mail their cash.

Ben interrupted: "Leon, why are you telling me this?"

"Because I'm settin' up a student support group and want you to front the thing. You're a professor. They got to do what you say. I'll write up what you tell them."

"No thanks."

"I'll pay you good money."

"You don't have good money, Leon. It's all bad money. I don't want any of it." Leon fumed and fled.

Ben lived quietly with *The Cantos* and Sophia. At night he read *Mad Magazine* to stay sane.

The Cantos, Eliot and lost generation writers in Europe consumed Ben's many years at Braynerd unless phone calls drew him back to the hills. Connie called to say Tuffy fell in the barn pitching hay and hurt her hip. Connie scheduled a family sit-down and said he better show up. Ben first went to her hospital room and visited Tuffy. She had refused an operation and decided to put her fate in God's hands. Her tight smile told him that subject was closed. When he entered the hospital's antiseptic meeting room Ben found the Doss crew on alert. Cletis, Cutie, Donnalou, and Leon waited while

Connie paced. Ben waved hello and took a seat. Then Connie took over.

"Here's the way it's gonna be. The doc says Tuffy can't do much physical stuff anymore, but we all know she'll do it anyhow if we don't stop her. So that's what we're gonna do, even if she gets pissed off. She'll bitch about it all the time, but I ain't comin' here every day 'cause she hurt herself doin' shit she can't do anymore. Cletis and I made a list of all the stuff we got to do for her and with her. We'll hire help for some of it. Donnalou will keep the list current. If you can't make it for your turn get somebody to cover. That's your problem so don't call Donnalou about it. Finding your subs ain't her job.

"Ben, you got a car and gas money so you'll have stuff to do. Mostly paperwork and handling her money. Randall at the bank knows you're in charge of that."

Leon interrupted: "I can help with some of that if you want, Ben."

Connie: "You're not helpin' with her goddamn money, Leon. Tend to the shit on your list 'cause I'll be checkin' on you. Every time you don't show up or have someone cover for you, I'll go to your lot and set fire to one of your cars. I'll burn the sumbitch to the ground."

"You can't do that. It's illegal."

"Most of those cars were stolen out of state. Make sure the cops and insurance boys know that when you report the fire. They'll have questions for you when they get a hit on the VIN. This is all to protect Tuffy so I'm not fuckin' around, Leon. Now do what you're told."

After Tuffy's disabilities worsened and she moved into a nursing home, Judge Cody talked the county judges into awarding her a special citizenship award. The reason became clear when he spoke about her during the presentation ceremony. Cody took his place at the lectern and began to speak in that raspy voice everyone recognized.

"I know most of you, but not all of you. I'm Judge Cody, and Tuffy told me to be quick about it so that's what you're gettin'. I'm a blunt man, too blunt, my wife says, but here it is. We are here to pay tribute to one of the most remarkable women God ever gave this world. Most of you know when you went to Tuffy with a burden

Tuffy Doss Citizenship Award

you couldn't carry she picked it up and helped tote it. When people came to court with a problem the law couldn't fix I called Tuffy for help and got it. When Tuffy found a wrong she put it right. If nobody would stand up with her she stood alone. All of this may surprise some of you because Tuffy kept the countless kindnesses she bestowed between her and God. When nursing homes had a dying person with no family to comfort them Tuffy became their family. When children needed help they became her kids. She was dealt some bad hands in life, but Tuffy never complained. I could go on for days about this good woman, but you know where I stand. I've never been emotional, but I am now so I better shut up." Tuffy smiled from her wheelchair and nodded okay.

Wesley and Ben walked out of the auditorium and into trees surrounding the packed parking lot. "Isn't it odd that in many ways she raised both of us, and we never knew all this," Ben said. This led to many shared reflections about similarities of their lives. Some sweet spots. Some sour notes. A lot of should haves but didn't. At the end Ben regretted that the moments passed so quickly and had been so long in coming.

I Met This Girl

Wesley played in the Ivy League after academic excellence at Saint Thomas Aquinas Academy. Cutie followed him as best she could by phone. Ben also arranged for Wesley's term at Oxford. Both wanted to explore the Bodleian Library together and French connections of the modernist American expatriates during the 20s and 30s. In Europe they shared experiences that drew them closer and made them more tolerant of each other. Invitations for Cutie to join them only drew excuses. She had become comfortable letting them do it their way.

During Wesley's first year of law school at Northwestern, he showed up at Ben's Braynerd office. Something significant had come up. "Well, out with it," Ben said after his greeting.

"Still stingy with words."

"Already using lawyer deflections."

"Well, I met this girl. You're familiar with that line because you've read every novel in print. I need your advice."

"Have you talked to Cutie and Connie about this?"

"No. I need your help before talking to them."

"Why?"

"Mom will be intensely jealous and completely unfair. I don't want Connie putting Rebekah in a choke hold if she sides with Mom."

"Points taken. Tell me about this girl."

"We met at the art institute. She is a year younger than me, has a BA from U of C and is interning there for an MFA. Rebekah is highly intelligent, classy, attractive and from a prominent Chicago family. Her dad is senior partner at a prestigious law firm in the city. Her mom is at best bi-polar and at worst a lethal viper. Rebekah has several successful siblings. She is not a spoiled snob, but Mom will not believe me when I tell her that. Since I have a peasant's pedigree her mother will object to the wedding and try everything to sabotage it. Things will jump ugly on her side from the git. On my side, Mom will reject her unseen and unheard. Unless, of course, my godfather steps up with an offer she can't refuse."

"Is Rebekah the one and only and equally certain about you?"

"Yes and yes."

"Have you made her a promise you must keep?"

"I have."

"Then burn the boats and fight."

"I agree and need you out front."

"How?"

"If you meet Rebekah and approve, Mom and Connie will give her a fair shake. Their love for you and trust in your judgement will overcome all else. Once they get to know Rebekah she'll win them over. I am profoundly in love with Rebekah and will be forever. She is a good person. All she needs is a chance."

"Arrange a time and place for lunch in the city. I'll meet the two of you there."

When Ben walked into the small café he saw that Wesley had low-balled Rebekah. She was strikingly attractive with dark auburn hair, a fit body and unfathomable smile. She stood and stuck out her hand. "Is it to be Dr. Hart or Ben?"

"Always Ben. Never Dr. Hart."

"With me it's Beka or Rebekah, your pick."

"I pick Rebekah."

She appeared apprehensive, and Ben said nothing to relax her. It worked.

"As you can see I'm a nervous wreck."

"Why?"

"You know exactly why. But I'll itemize for you. I'm sitting with a man I am desperate to impress. A complete mystery to his family, including his godson. Brilliant. Extraordinarily difficult if not impossible. Does not do small talk or tolerate bullshit. How am I doing so far."

"Okay. Let's order."

She began again without prompting after the waitress took their orders. "For the record, I am marrying Wesley no matter what. We will raise our kids and be together until death do us part. That will happen no matter what you want or anybody else wants. Period. But I would like your blessing. We both would."

"Have you talked to your family about this?"

"They know we're seeing each other regularly but don't know we're living in sin. Everybody likes Wesley, except Mother, because he's not a Chicago scion. I'm trying to figure out what to do about her. Right now I'm worried about his family, specifically his mom and Connie. He thinks they could be a problem."

"They won't. I'll tend to it."

Rebekah put down her fork: "Are you serious?"

"Do I look serious?"

"Yes."

"What else is on your mind?"

"I was so nervous about this. Wesley, are we all good here?"

"Looks like it."

"Ben, I am so thrilled and thankful. Do you want some chit-chat or can I run some wedding issues by you."

"Run 'em."

"We're thinking about eloping for several reasons. If we have a massive Chicago wedding I guarantee you during our vows Mother will collapse in the aisle faking a massive heart attack to stop the ceremony. I'm not exaggerating. She will create a catastrophe one way or another. Wesley says the gathering of wealthy Yankees in one spot drinking heavily may attract a used car dealer named Leon with blank sales contracts and cash to make change. He may even bring lap dancers to work the crowd. We want to avoid both."

"Eloping is good."

"Terrific. Next is the cost. Mother and her wedding planner society friend will run up enormous bills somehow. I don't want your family to pay for anything."

"Can't help you there. Cutie will demand to pay our fair share. Wesley's dad is rich as it gets in the hills. Let Wesley mediate the issue after a date is set. I'll back him."

"I owe you forever."

Ben called Connie the next day: "We need to talk."

"About what?"

"About Wesley's fiancée. I had lunch with them yesterday and was impressed. Rebekah loves him dearly and is good people. You can tell."

"Does Cutie know about this?"

"No. We're going to need your help with Cutie. Rebekah is beautiful, classy, well-educated, from a prominent Chicago family."

"So she's the rich bitch Cutie has always been afraid of, who'll shame her and steal her baby."

"Exactly. Connie, they are getting married no matter what. Totally committed. I like her. Cutie should give her a chance. That's all they're asking for. We've got to help Cutie see that. It's not right to fight them or us. I don't want to deal with it, particularly if it wedges me against Cutie or you. The three of us run too deep to let that happen."

"That ain't ever gonna happen," Connie said. "I need to think about how we handle it. If we both do a sit-down she may think we're double-teaming her. She'll get worked up and start walkin' sideways. Let me call her about it. Tell her Wesley loves the girl. You like her a lot. I agree that we meet her and see what we think. If Cutie throws a hissy I'll tell her to shut the fuck up. It's gonna happen with or without her. If the girl is no good we'll help Cutie hide the body. But if she's a keeper we won't let Cutie run her off without giving the girl a chance. That ain't right. I'll back off then. She'll start in on you right away, but that's your problem. You okay with that?"

"Yep."

Cutie called the next day. "How are you doin' Sweetie?" she purred. Oh shit, Ben thought, Cutie brought her A game.

"I'm okay. Assume you talked to Connie. So how are you?"

"Guess I'm wondering why this girl didn't want to meet me before everybody else."

"Cutie, I know where you're headed, and I'm not going there with you. Rebekah is a good girl and perfect fit for Wesley. We should be happy for him and us."

"What will she think about our kin?"

"The same thing we think. But that doesn't matter. If you run her off he'll go with her. They plan to have kids. So your grandchildren too. You have to decide if you want to lose all of them or make it work. The rest is irrelevant. That's my take."

Wesley called the day after that. "What's going on," he said.

"I'm trying to spend a quiet weekend with Proust. Despite the cluster fuck you've gotten me into."

"I should have mentioned that Rebekah is on the extension. She wants to talk to you."

"Howdy Rebekah. What's up?"

"I know you're pissed. But I need help. Connie called Wesley to say we've got to have a sit-down. Please describe the preferred shape of that."

"Give them home field for comfort. You and Wesley go to Grinder's Switch and have a cheeseburger at Dotty's café. Do not dress up or down. Be open and honest. Connie won't say much. Never does. Cutie will behave. Wesley can fill the holes. Be nothing but you. They'll respect that."

"How can I ever repay you?"

"You can't."

Two weeks later Wesley called with good reviews about the sit-down. The family asked a lot of questions about life in Chicago. They learned Rebekah was working at an abandoned animal rescue facility shoveling dogshit for minimum wage. She talked to them about changing her career to something having to do with helping needy creatures. Rebekah told them her mother was a high society snob they would hate for good reasons. But not to worry. None of the kids liked her either. Wesley took them to see Tuffy. Cletis and Donnalou were waiting with her for the introduction. Tuffy settled the matter when they came in. Though hobbling, she walked toward Rebekah with open arms. "Honey, come hug what's left of your husband's grandma." She did, and Rebekah was visibly moved by this validation.

As everyone descended around the big kitchen table Donnalou said, "I'm gonna go pick strawberries for our shortcake."

Rebekah stood: "Do you mind if I help? I've never seen a strawberry patch."

"Come on."

The family watched from a window as Rebekah and Donnalou crawled down dirt rows on their knees picking berries. "Wesley," Cletis said, "you got a keeper there." Everyone nodded, including Cutie.

After Rebekah's big win in Grinder's Switch, she decided to announce the future wedding to her family. That would be tricky given her unstable mother. Rebekah insisted that Wesley keep Ben fully informed of her progress with periodic phone calls. They both developed a growing appreciation for her cleverness. Rebekah's mother would never agree to an elopement. It would suggest an unsavory concealment of some sort and deny her mother many opportunities for social spotlighting. So Rebekah went at it in a way that provided a measure of revenge for all the unhappiness her mother brought to her and the siblings. Her mother had determined it would be the greatest wedding in Chicago history. Rebekah said nothing to the contrary.

Rebekah slyly picked Connie as the Doss wedding liaison. The final phase of Rebekah's plan began after Connie landed in Chicago. Rebekah's mother demanded that Rebekah take Wesley's aunt to the posh wedding shop that socialites used to dominate their kids' nuptials. On the way there Connie confirmed that Rebekah had a list of all the stuff they needed. Connie mentioned that she had kept her wedding expenses to about a hundred dollars, including cost of the campsite's honeymoon tent. Rebekah smiled discreetly.

When they walked in the store a hostess rushed to the office to tell Margaret Whiting, the store's owner and a high society doyen, that Rebekah had arrived. Margaret announced that she and Rebekah's mother already had agreed on every stage of the wedding. Margaret cast aside all the choices on Rebekah's list with a condescending smirk.

Connie leaned over the counter. "Lady, you better shut the fuck up and listen hard." After hearing this, other customers evacuated. "This ain't gonna be a rich girl wedding because my folks ain't got the money to pay for our share of all the silly shit you wanna sell us. This is Rebekah's wedding. Whatever she wants is the way it's gonna be. So stop the high-steppin' and put all the stuff she wants in a big sack. Call her house so somebody can come get it and pay you. I'll give her my half. Come on, Rebekah, we better go 'fore I jump ugly on this bitch."

Margaret called Rebekah's mother immediately and insisted that the Sharpe's social standing would be destroyed unless she put a stop to the wedding. Mrs. Sharpe called her husband at his law office and demanded that he and their children come home for an emergency meeting. Otherwise, she would call for an ambulance because of her severe chest pains.

Rebekah arrived late because she stayed at the airport to have a beer with Connie. When she got home everyone, including her siblings, looked up warily from their seats at the dining room table. When Rebekah sat down her father asked what happened. When Rebekah repeated what Connie said to Margaret verbatim, smiles surfaced. Until their father said, "Now that's one hell of a closing argument." Then laughter broke out. Their mother exploded. "We must cancel the wedding immediately. I'll handle the details." Mr. Sharpe interrupted: "Rebekah, do you want to cancel the wedding?"

"No, Father. The wedding is on. We'll elope. We saved up enough money."

"Okay, that's settled. Wesley is a brilliant young man with admirable personal qualities. I welcome him into our family."

This brought Rebekah's older brother Bernard to his feet. "I agree. I consider Wesley an excellent choice. I'm happy for you. Margaret eliminated everything Clarissa and I wanted in our wedding. She ruined it for us. We despise the woman."

Mrs. Sharpe gasped for air, clutched her chest, moaned beneath her pity mask and limped out of the room. Everyone watched her exit with theatrical flair but said nothing They had seen this act before. When Bernard said, "I want to hire Connie for my union negotiations," they howled.

Me Too, Buddy, Me Too

When Cutie wouldn't turn back toward him, Ben began to sob, attempting to hide his face. It didn't work. Cletis said, "I know, buddy, me too. … I know, buddy, me too." Cutie had inoperable cancer. She went to a hospital in Texas and learned that breast cancer had spread to her brain. The family didn't find out until she entered a local Hospice. Little could be done except diminish her pain with morphine. When Ben walked into her room, only a faint smile and whisper said hello. He sat on the side of Cutie's bed, hugged her, and cried. Cutie shushed him and held his hands before speaking. "Sweetie, I'm okay with what's coming. I'm more worried about you and Wesley right now. I met with him yesterday, and he promised to watch over you. And you watch over him. Rebekah came with him. That girl is true blue and tough."

Ben had asked Cletis and Connie to wait in the hall. Donnalou, Rebekah and Wesley were there. "You got good people ridin' with you now," Cutie said. "You'll do okay."

He began to cry again. But she interrupted. "Sweetie, I need you to stop cryin' and listen. I got a list. Will you do that for me?"

"I'll try," he said, but couldn't see her clearly for the tears.

"First, I told the doctor not to do anything more. The chemo was making me sick, and I don't want to go out that way. Wesley took care of all the paperwork. If anything comes up he'll handle it. I just want a graveside prayer. That's all. Daggart is too sick to come." She paused to ponder something. "We've been down a lot of rough roads haven't we, Sweetie. You and my boy are the loves of my life." Cutie paused, sighed, and turned away from him. "These are the hardest words I'll ever say, but I want you to leave now and not come back. I don't want you to see me like this and what I'm gonna look like from now on. Now please go."

"No. I can't. I'd rather die here with you."

"You got to, Sweetie. Wesley did it for me yesterday. You can today. Do it for me. I'm begging you, Sweetie. I'm begging."

He broke down completely and couldn't stand. Cletis came in, steadied Ben and began his mantra. He had observed from the hall, waiting for this moment. Connie and Donnalou walked in and hugged Ben front and back. Walking into the hall Ben saw Wesley frozen in time and space. Though sobbing, Rebekah held him tight, full-length and rock solid. Ben kept his promise. A few days later Connie ended Cutie's ordeal with morphine. Ben remained dry-eyed at the burial. He walked with Wesley who carried Cutie's ashes to the Doss homeplace where her spirit would roam forever beneath a gigantic oak tree.

The tree's enormous size reminded them of her forever presence in their lives.

Ben then told Wesley he was leaving Braynerd. Was coming home. Had important things to do. Wesley had questions. But knew some of the answers already.

"It's good to have you back home," Connie said. But her attitude changed when she swung open the moving truck's back door. "Goddammit Ben, this thing is full of books. How many books are in here?"

"Not sure."

"There's thousands. I'm not helping you unload these fucking books. You'll have to do it yourself or hire some Mexicans."

Cletis broke in: "I'll send some hands to do that. We need to go in and talk about all the information we gathered that you wanted. There's a whole lot and then some."

Doss Holding Company, DHC, was conceived that afternoon. Ben became capo without applying for the job. He had worked toward his concept for many years. Reading about and researching vast areas of business law and finance. Daggart's empire had gone into Wesley's trust, which Ben and Wesley controlled. Wesley's brother-

in-law Bernard had used his investment management group to turn Ben's cash into a substantial investment portfolio. Rebekah's family wealth was buying additional land for an animal habitat (the Hab) she established. Cletis and Connie had invested family money in more regional timberland and farms. Connie managed timber operations. Cletis oversaw farms and several integrated enterprises. Sharpe family marketing contacts were working on a proposal for Ben's approval that would expand the county's business opportunities connected to the Hab. Ben was in charge of it all, but bigness was giving him headaches.

Penalty Stroke

Ben saw Pene sitting across the room in a folding chair staring at him. "I can explain this if you give me a chance," he said.

"Can't wait."

"The Ferris wheel collapsed. You died. But my prayers about meeting you in Heaven were answered."

"Several problems with that, Ben. You weren't praying. You were laughing at me. Another is if you want the highway to Heaven, you better find an exit ramp immediately."

"My God. A sarcastic wag. And you used to be so shy and sweet."

"I planned to say something encouraging about how good you look despite the surgery. But you look awful. Throughout life you have gorged on all manner of excess, and God finally brought the check."

"Do we call for the wailing women."

"What obscure source are you quoting?"

"The prophet Jeremiah. With your bedside manner no wonder you never made the cheerleading squad."

"Never tried out. Couldn't see myself shaking a pompom and my ass for a bunch of randy schoolboys. Do you want to know why you're here?"

"Yep."

"You had a stroke and bad bleed at Dotty's. The police chief got there first and called an ambulance. Then he called Randall Miller at the bank to find out who is next of kin. They thought you were dying. Cletis, Donnalou, Connie and the kids are at the lake fishing. Leon is in Reno. Randall knows I'm in town so he called me to keep from upsetting Tuffy. I went to Dotty's to check on you, and the chief put me in charge after I begged him not to. I tried to bribe him for a catch and release. But he refused my cash."

"Where am I?"

"Little Rock. Your surgery was exceptionally difficult. After checking around I decided this hospital was your best shot. They expect you to recover with minor damage. The neurologist says you may have long-term problems with vision, memory and cognition. But Ben, you damn near died. This is a win. You have to be patient and cooperate with these people. Your surgeon will come in with the team and explain it all. You'll stay in ICU for a few days. Don't you dare cut any of them with that sharp tongue. I mean it. If that happens I'll send Connie for an intervention."

Ben suddenly went mentally numb. Pene noticed. "What's wrong?" she asked, but he couldn't speak.

After a few seconds Ben returned to reality. "I don't know what happened. But I know I'm scared."

Pene sat on the bed and held him. "Any sane person would be. But you'll get better. I promise. I reached Wesley by phone. He is in the middle of negotiations with a big corporation about something important. He apologized profusely about this crisis landing in my lap and said he'll fly in from Chicago the second he wraps up. You should be proud of him. I know Cutie was, and she credited you for it. Rebekah called after Wesley got hold of her. She is volunteering for morning shifts when she gets back from some wild animal refuge in Central America. You need to rest now. Dennis stayed during the operation until we got the good news. He insisted I tell all of your minders to call him immediately if they need extra help."

"Thank him for me. Can you stay for a while?"

"I'll come back after lunch. We can catch up some."

He dozed until Pene returned with a cup of coffee for her, but none for him. "Where is mine?"

"No caffeine."

"Why?"

"Talk to your doctors during rounds. And let's get this straight from the start. I'll not put up with any bitching, self-pity, whining or temperamental outbursts. Is that clear?"

"Sounds clear. You haven't changed in at least two respects. The irritating bluntness and good looks. You are an attractive lady, always have been."

"Thanks, but that won't get you a cup of coffee. And put away all your tools. They won't fix what's broke between us."

"What I said is true on both counts. Tell me what happened after high school?"

"Okay, but only a few highlights. I got a BA at Arkansas and went to vet school at UT. Met my husband there. We bought out a clinic in South Carolina and moved into a beach house. Carter and I were successful financially, have two good sons, and managed well for more than 20 years. But an attractive young woman became director of the regional animal shelter and retained Carter as a consultant. Then things changed. She has the body of a Vegas hooker and a spoiled brat's personality. I knew something was wrong. I questioned Carter about her, and he made up elaborate lies he couldn't keep straight. When he agreed to attend a conference in Atlanta with her I surprised them in a hotel room. Filed for divorce immediately, and Carter began teary-eyed pleas about how it only happened once and would never happen again. When my boys found out they shunned him, and I couldn't help Carter regain their trust. They share my view about liars. Jeffrey is a former Marine infantry officer who is deputy chancellor at the state's renowned military academy. Cliff is a trauma surgeon. Both are straight arrows. Carter would have been better off slapping them with the truth than kissing them with lies."

"Ah, you have a remarkable recall of Russian proverbs."

"I wondered if you would recognize it. I've been saving it for years. You should be honored."

"Honored is not the word that comes to mind. So what are you doing now?"

"I'm a professor of veterinary science at South Carolina. I specialize in large animal surgery. Tough stuff. My boys live nearby. They have good marriages and great kids. I'm happy."

"Is there a man in your life?"

"A few. My sons. Their sons. Dennis and his sons. Larry died several years ago. That is all there ever will be. I'm done, Ben. Dennis and my boys say I am much too difficult to get along with anybody else. Your turn."

"Why were you in Grinder's Switch?"

"I come back occasionally when Dennis needs advice about vet issues. Actually, I advise his sons and daughters. They run the company now. They save up questions and ask me to bring answers. It gives me a chance to see everybody and solve some problems."

"When you see Dennis please tell him thanks for me. On our break-up day he displayed class and genuine concern. I appreciate and admire him."

"I'll tell him, and I'll tell you something that embarrasses me still. Dennis got angry with me that day about the way I acted, but I was furious. He urged me to show some grace and sympathy. It soon became clear that butt blister Darnell got you in the mess. When I learned the truth I went to Dennis to talk about it. He refused. Said I should talk to you about not defending someone I loved and taking the word of gossips and troublemakers instead. That was a bad place in my life. Couldn't swallow my pride. So I choked on it. What I'm trying to say is I handled my part poorly. I'm sorry."

Pene stayed for much of the afternoon and shared the happy and sad parts. When he looked at her and grinned Pene smiled. "What."

"I recalled the way you looked when you climbed off that Ferris wheel. Sweaty hair strung out all over your head. Face like a medieval death mask."

"Damn you. Nothing was funny about that. You don't even know the whole story."

"Tell me."

"While we were up there thinking we were going to die Karen wet her pants. It was disgusting. She couldn't stop. Some of it got on my pants, but then the wheel started going down. I made Lonnie give me his cardigan and wrapped it around my waist to hide the soaked part. Then I saw you laughing. If I had Dennis' deer rifle I would have put you down and done the time. That's why I rode home with them. I was terrified you would find out and tell somebody during one of your destructive moods."

Their long talk that day revealed newness in each other and the realization that oldness was long gone.

Ben slept most of the time and stirred amid checkups, tests and bland meals with over-cooked Brussels sprouts. He woke up two days later to find Rebekah watching from a recliner. She bounded toward him. "Wesley and I are worn out from worry. Do you need anything?" After those words she kissed him loudly on both cheeks and hugged his shoulders.

"Just good company, and I have it now. Can you stay for a while?"

"Absolutely. Wesley is coming after he finishes bailing out the asset acquisition team Chicago sent down here. They can't get anything done. Said people here are nuts."

"Well, they got that part right. So what's going on?"

"The conglomerate's plans were going nowhere in the fast lane. God, I'm beginning to talk like you. That's not a good thing, is it?"

"No. Definitely not."

"Well, anyhow, Wesley's in Grinder's Switch trying to get things back on track. He has been named chief operating officer of a Chicago corporate spin-off to run regional operations in Arkansas. My father told their board chairman, a golfing buddy, that Wesley was the fixer they needed. Before he got involved, their people thought ignorant hillbillies were rollover whores who would quickly take their cash for land and property corporate wanted. But it wasn't turning out that way.

'One prospect wouldn't sell because he didn't know them and worried their check would bounce. An owner of a crucial piece of land said they sounded like Yankees. And his great grandfather had been killed unfairly by Yankees at Shiloh when he tried to run off. A prospect named Wheezer Doss wouldn't talk because the barbershop said newcomers might have the clap and give it to schoolgirls."

That one broke up both Rebekah and Ben. He sipped water. Rebecca couldn't stop laughing.

While Rebekah laughed, Wesley sat with Curtis Doss, a distant cousin, at his kitchen table in Grinder's Switch, along with two purchasing agents. Wesley wore his country boy mask. "Curtis, you know Tuffy helped raise me, and I live by her words: 'If it ain't true don't say it. If it ain't right don't do it.'"

"Wesley, I never heard a bad word about you from anybody," Curtis interrupted. "Everybody knows you're a good man and real smart. And you're one of us."

"Thanks. So please listen to my thoughts about this. We're making you a fair, respectful offer. Don't risk another year working your guts out without a nickel left after paying the bills. You've already had one heart attack. Cash out and buy an FDIC-insured CD at the bank. With a guaranteed payment and no risk of losing your money. Then lean back in the recliner and listen to Dizzy and Peewee call the Cardinals games.

"Get legal help to review the contract and help with tax and estate planning. Make your nephew Randall, the best bank president we've ever had, get his home office to send its lawyer for consults. Tell them they got to do it for free to get the CD business. There are a lot of folks here who can benefit from this. But you're the key man. You'll have to be lead mule till lay-by. Now call our kin and neighbors. The more folks you get the more bargaining power you got. You know how that works. This ain't your first trip to the mule barn."

Curtis signed his contract and agreed to take the lead. Wesley went to the bank with his agents for introductions and to explain the plan to Randall. He enthusiastically agreed to help since the new business would increase his value to the bank's board. Before they departed, Randall cornered the agents: "Just so ya'll know. Wesley is one of the state's most powerful and respected leaders." This was bullshit, but Randall grew up on a cattle ranch and knew how to pitch it. Their success rang in Chicago immediately.

By the time Wesley finished up and arrived at Ben's hospital room, his godfather and Rebekah were napping.

Homecoming

Cletis knocked on Ben's hospital door the next day and rushed in. "Ben, you gotta hear this. The reason I can't reach Leon is he, Langston and Preston are in a Mexican jail."

"How'd they manage that?"

"All I know is what Leon told Connie when he bribed a guard to get a phone call. Apparently the Feds were after them for a lot of stuff, stealing campaign donations, bribery, tax evasion and such. After they found out the Feds were getting close, all three headed to Matamoros, just across the Mexican border."

"How did they end up in jail?"

"Leon said they got in trouble because he swapped their leased car and some boot for a used Jaguar XKE in Brownsville. Leon said he could roll back the mileage and make a killing on the Jag. Cops found it at a house across the Rio Grande where the three were hidin'. When the Mexican cops raided them, Langston got in trouble first. A Federale's sniffer dog started barking at Langston. He tried to kick the dog in the head. When he turned to run, the dog bit off a chunk of his ass. He's in a filthy clinic where nurses use the same needle for everybody's shots. Leon claimed the three were set up because word got out that Langston was running for President. Preston had two large suitcases full of hundred dollar bills. Mexican cops called him a drug kingpin and kept all his money for evidence."

"So why is he calling Connie?"

"To borrow money he'll never get," Cletis said and transitioned abruptly.

"Donnalou came up with a plan I need to run by you."

"Run it."

"Connie will keep helping Tuffy. Rebekah will check on you when Donnalou can't. I asked Portis Doss to loan us his son Travis to help me look after farm stuff. Travis has worked for me before and knows what to do. Wesley said he would handle paperwork and check on you. Donnalou helped run an outpatient clinic in Howard County before we married. She worked with a young woman named Dumpling, who is excellent with sick people. I want your permission to hire her to take care of you day-to-day for a stretch when we get you home. I told Connie if she scares off Dumpling I'll strangle her ass in the church parking lot."

"Sounds fair. Hire Dumpling. We'll make it work."

Dumpling came to his room the next morning about an hour before the hospital planned to release him. "Hi, I'm Dumpling, Mr. Hart. Can I help you get ready to go?"

"Real soon. Just waiting on the paperwork. What's your given name?"

"Susan, but call me Dumpling. That's been my name since I was a kid."

"Okay, Dumpling it is. I'm Ben, not Mr. Hart. I know from Donnalou that you were raised around here. Tell me a little about yourself."

"Yeah. Now I own a flower shop here. My daddy was from Grinder's Switch. He died when an 18-wheeler hit him head-on. Daddy died instantly. The other guy was stoned on meth and lived. Judge Cody got us a large check from the insurance company. That helps me take care of Mama's nursing home bills. My cousin Terry does most of the work at the shop, handles the money and paperwork. When Donnalou called about you I was interested because it gives me something important to do, and I can earn a little money. I hope you're okay with what I'm charging. Connie told me it's a fair price, and I didn't need to talk to you about it. But I should."

"No need. If Connie says we're good, we're good."

When Ben arrived at his house with Dumpling and Wesley, he saw mad women staring at him. Connie, Donnalou and Rebekah looked immensely unhappy. Everyone walked in after proforma greetings and reviewed the mess Ben created. Unkempt rooms, dirty floors, unwashed clothes, books piled everywhere, rotting food in the fridge, dirty plates and dishes stacked in the sink.

Wesley chose to disarm Connie before she got her hands around Ben's throat and choked him till twilight. "Several points to start with," he said. "Ya'll agreed that I would take charge of this disaster. I expect you to keep your word. Ben has turned this house into a pigsty. But let's focus on fixing the problem, not complaining about it. Ben is moving back in, and Dumpling will be his minder. That means she is the adult in complete charge. If Ben has a problem with that he should complain to Connie.

"Dumpling has our full support, and this message is for her: You were not hired to be the garbage collector. We'll all help you clean this up now, but don't let him ever do this again. Travis will assist with repairs and maintenance. Adjustments will be made as needed on the fly."

Travis helped a lot when Terry, Dumpling's attractive and bright cousin, began bringing lunch from

Dotty's. The first time Travis saw her pull in he walked over to offer a hand and warmed to her bright smile. Since he started making sure his chores lasted until she arrived, Terry brought his lunch too. They ate in his pickup. Until Dumpling thought she saw the cab rocking.

"Ya'll come inside and eat with the rest of us," she told them. Dumpling tried to keep an eye on them. But it became difficult because they took breaks in the barn to chat.

Dumpling called for a sit-down. "If ya'll are in love that's a good thing. But you must always respect each other. Always means always in every way. You can't be in a barn loft doin' the dandy like randy teenagers. That's not how God wants his gift to be given. I know you'll do what you're gonna do. But you'll not do it here." So they did, but not there. Several months later Travis and Terry pleaded with Dumpling to be a witness for their nuptials. She agreed, and it made all of them feel good.

Ben's relationship with Dumpling deepened after a few months. One frigid night she found him cold and shaking. Dumpling put her hand on his forehead. "You're freezing. What happened?"

"I don't know. I got up to pee and got chills. Did we replace the electric blanket that won't work?"

"No. I was supposed to get a new one but forgot. I'm so sorry."

"Don't worry about it. I'll tough it out until tomorrow."

"No. It might cause other problems." She paused. "I've only got on my nightgown, but I'm gonna get under your covers and try to keep you warm with body heat. If you get happy fingers I'll break all ten of 'em. You got that?"

"Got that." He felt her warm, soft, abundant body slide in. The thin gown filtered out very little of her anatomy and the warmth it provided. Dumpling stayed the night, and Ben told her in the morning to forget the electric blanket. She laughed. He hoped. On cold nights Dumpling joined him in bed as a medical precaution. Her rules remained in force until they didn't. Their comfort with each other soon grew into something greater.

When they snuggled in bed one night she said, "Am I right in thinking something good is going on here?"

"Yes."

"I didn't plan for this."

"And?"

"I'm afraid it will ruin our relationship. When I take up with a man it ends in a mess."

"Maybe they weren't as warm and cuddly as me."

"Ben, you're pretty near awful sometimes. But at least you don't try to make me think it's always my fault. This may make you mad, but I talked to Connie and Rebekah two days ago about us. I wanted their advice."

"Was that necessary?"

"Yes, because you're so strange. I don't always know what you're talking about or who you are. I've never known a man like you. Rebekah and you are alike in education and smarts. Connie loves you like a big sister. I asked them how they would feel if we get serious. They're okay with it."

"Okay. Now that everybody else is okay, are we okay?"

"I'm okay. Are you?"

"I'm okay. Unless this conversation continues. If it does I may stick my head in the oven to end it."

She laughed. "The three of us had a long girls' lunch at Dotty's after the crowd thinned and spent a lot of it laughing about you. Rebekah is a lady, but tough and straight ahead. When I asked her about you, she said you're a pain in the ass but worth it. I told her I knew that already. Connie said if we go steady to keep rat poison handy. Despite the teasing they love you a lot."

"Are we going steady?"

"Yeah, but I have to be careful. Folks in my church are watchin'. I've been divorced twice. Some already think I'm a loose woman. I'm claiming I must be here 24-7 because we're worried you'll have a seizure or another stroke. If that happens you've got to get to the ER immediately or a lot of harm can be done that can't be undone. But they're Christians with their rules."

"Dumpling, you are a Christian of conscience. They are not. They live according to rules they made up, not loving hearts. Most are wearing Jesus masks to hide the truth. Ignore them."

"Why do you use that thing about people wearing masks all the time?"

"Because it's a universal response for human protection and manipulation. When people run into a situation that might reveal their true selves the masks go on. It can even be automatic, and they may not realize they're doing it. You don't fully understand this because you're real all the time."

"You're making me sound too good. You'll be disappointed."

"Not as long as you don't threaten me like Connie does."

"Boy, Connie is a tough nut to crack. I can't figure out how she and Rebekah got so close."

"It's partly to do with the fact that Rebekah was emotionally abused by a vicious, unstable mother. Wesley says she's a tyrant. Then along came Connie. She taught Rebekah how to deal with tyrants."

Before they got up to start supper Ben baited her. "The first time you got in bed with me did you do it to warm me up in two ways?"

"Ben, never ask an honest woman to tell her secrets. She might have to lie." After that they grilled the chicken.

Family Affairs

People in high and low places sought Ben's advice about various matters. He complained constantly, but Dumpling said it was a sign of respect and to stop whining. Rebekah gave him monthly truck-window tours of her expanding Hab. When a niece or nephew asked for a job during summer break, she cleared it with Ben before hiring them. Rebekah's niece Drew became her de facto Number Two after graduating from Georgetown.

Rebekah asked Ben for a greasy cheeseburger date at Dotty's to talk about stuff. She began after swallowing her first chunk and wiping grease off her chin. "We've got to talk about a bunch of things. My family is making unsolicited financial and personal commitments to our work here. I've made it clear to everybody that I will always be connected to DHC. They want to know what that means."

"It means whatever you want it to," Ben said.

"Ben, please help me understand. You're running this complicated financial empire, and nobody but you understands how it all works. Actually, Wesley does. But he insists I talk to you about it. I hear from a reliable source that Wesley, Bernard, you and Randall are buying regional banks through a new LLC. So we're into that business."

"I don't consider banks a business. They're weapons. Money is like plasma. You need it. Banks can loan it to you. Or not. Charge you a fortune for it. Or not. Pay you interest on deposits. Or nothing. Help you when you're falling. Or say no. "It's all about power and control."

"I need to read your mentor Machiavelli. But right now I want to be certain my family's participation and new hires pose no threat to our kin here. I talked to Wesley, Cletis, Connie and Dumpling about it. They all point to you since you control it all, even if you won't admit it.

"Is it my turn now?"

"Yes, and thanks for not interrupting me the way you usually do." She took another bite of burger.

"Rebekah, you and Wesley are the heavyweights in our scrum. I know you're advising others when asked. Your judgment is sound and solutions workable. I'm comfortable with what you're doing so keep on doing it. That's it. Short meeting. The way I like 'em."

"Is that all," Rebekah said while attempting to chew.

"Yep."

"I haven't finished my burger."

"So take it with you."

"No. We're not finished here. My Father and Bernard bought a hill on Spring River because they know about the trout fishing there. Cletis took them a couple of times. And the quail hunting. And the duck hunting. And other pathetic, male-bonding bullshit with guns and dead animals. If they hurt anything on the Hab I'll borrow Connie's sniper rifle. She taught me how to use it. My family is building a compound with huge rustic houses, a swimming pool, tennis court and other amenities. Father wants to spend part of his retirement here, probably to get far away from Mother because she'll never come. My brothers, sisters, their kids, cousins, friends and business associates plan to freeload as much as possible. Are you okay with that. And what about everybody else."

"Yes. If I'm okay everybody will be."

"I need to hire some expensive people for complicated tax planning, vet specialties, scientific research, federal agency compliance, etcetera. Drew and I need help bad."

"I'll write the check."

"Thanks, Ben, but no. My sister's marketing group has enlisted the help of tree-hugging congressmen. They are spreading the word and passing the hat. Wesley and I have been penciled in for a couple of fund-raising dinners in D.C."

"Anything else."

"Yes. I saved the worst for last. This may piss you off, but I don't want any of my Sharpe kin knowing about or being involved in some of the things you and Connie handle for all of us. I'm being hypocritical because I know I've benefited from it. But Drew and I want to draw a red line. Just the two of us on the red side. The rest of our Sharpes on the other side. Can you live with that."

"Yes, but can you? You and Drew may have to deal with nasty stuff."

"No, Ben. You and Connie will. The way you always do."

Their conversation bothered Ben, so he called Connie for a sit-down at his home office. "Rebekah needs to bring in some high-end help. All sorts of suits. DHC may need some too. We own outright or in part about twenty profitable businesses and tens of thousands of acres. We're stretched too thin."

"What's first."

"The two of us. The bad stuff we do when we have to. We can't let that leave the room."

"People already know how we settle up. That's why they never get crosswise. Rebekah and Wesley know about the shit we do."

"How."

"She came to me about Pete Baxter. That asshole was poachin' on Hab land. She asked me about goin' to cops for help. Too slow or not at all, I said. I told Pete to stop, and he told me to fuck off. I knee-capped the prick with a bat. His son Dither came at me till I pulled my Colt and racked a round. They don't poach her anymore. Rebekah knows why Pete uses a crutch. Rebekah is kin and a fighter. She knows we only hurt them who hurt ours. Wesley is razor sharp and lawyer cold. Don't worry about them."

"She plans for the Hab to become an internationally recognized resource for vet training, scientific research and student participation in animal husbandry," Ben added. "Plus, I want a tourist draw to benefit the county. She'll need a lot of people that Dosses may not like."

"Ben, folks are warmin' up to the hot money we're bringin' in. The Finches are buying that run-down motel on Cleaver Ridge and rebuilding it into a two-story hotel with a bar and cafe. Dotty's son is doubling the size of their place to keep up. Folks around here always wanted to amount to somethin'. We're helpin' 'em do it."

Ben nodded. "Cletis is training Travis' brother Trace and niece Katie to help manage all the real estate, agri and commercial. He made Katie get a degree in agricultural management. Their problem now is getting more farm labor."

"Sit still and don't jump up on me," Connie said. "Preston's Mexican capo Tio pulled up to my truck when I was watchin' some cutters." Ben bristled. But Connie stared him down. "He said to let him know if we need some loggers or farm help. Said he's got good people who need legit jobs. He promised their mamas he'd keep 'em out of the drug trade and get 'em an education. Sounds like his kin."

"Why didn't he come to me."

"Said you're way too smart and dangerous to deal with."

"Now that's rich. He's killed more people than the Luftwaffe."

"Tio is different, and I understand him better than you do. I see him a lot because he lives in our county with his family and lots of relatives. You've seen his big spread, Casa Verde. I keep an eye out. None of them cause trouble. The principal says their kids are smart and well-behaved. Study hard. They all run together. Family is everything, and he rules it. Like Don Corleone, Tio keeps his business separate. I told him I'd talk to you about workin' some of his people. But no drug problems. Ever. We won't have it. Tio said not to worry. He won't have it either with his people."

"If you want, hire a few cutters and let's see what turns up. But we must never have anything to do with his drug business. No slippage. Ever."

"For sure. I made that real clear to him"

"Does he understand."

"Sure. But he'll always try to get his nose under our tent. That's his nature. Leave Tio to me. You keep dealing with all the big stuff I don't understand."

"On a different personnel matter, Terry is now a CPA and an MBA."

Connie shrugged: "Don't know why Terry went to school for all those years. She's been handling our stuff just fine."

"Connie, Terry is like the rest of us, stretched too far. I want her to reorganize and oversee accountants in our entities and give me consolidated financials. She'll need to hire some professionals. I want her in charge, not grinding numbers. I'm naming her Chief Financial Officer of DHC if you're okay with it. We can trust her to help cover up the holes where we bury the bodies."

"Okay. Your call."

Things never go the way they should because human nature won't have it. When the day arrived for several DHC scholarship kids to celebrate their passage to college, Dumpling made Ben attend the event. As he swiftly consumed his punch and snickerdoodle in order to leave early Ben surveilled people in the school auditorium. He studied Rebekah and Travis talking, attempting to look distant to disguise being close. It puzzled him until his red light flashed. Dumpling noticed Ben's discomfort and exited with him. After Dumpling brought full mugs to the kitchen table, he said, "How long have Rebekah and Travis been too close."

"Don't rightly know. Connie saw them going at it in his truck one night and asked me what to do. I've been too heartsick and mad to say anything. I should have told you, but I chickened out every time I started to. Connie got smokin' hot when she told me, but I made her promise to let you handle it."

"Who else knows?"

"Not sure. But I don't think Wesley has any idea. He's too busy puttin' out company fires and tending to all sorts of troubles."

The next morning they sat at the same table with the same mugs and same problem. But Ben's mind was clear. "I want to meet with Rebekah this afternoon with you present. You'll need to be silent because I'll say dreadful things. I intend to scare them so close to death they'll see Satan smiling. They'll go around me to you for help. That's the plan. Questions?"

"I see what you're up to. But please keep your temper in check. What's that you say about revenge?"

"It's a dish best served cold."

"Right. So stay cool. I'll call Rebekah for a sit-down."

That afternoon Rebekah arrived in a good mood. After a polite hello they settled in his office. She took the chair across from Ben's desk. Dumpling's bottom filled the rocker seat.

"So what's up."

"What's up is someone we trust saw you and Travis fucking in his pickup."

Her face turned snow white, then red. "I may throw up."

"Not on my rug. Go out in the yard."

She gasped. "Will you listen?"

"You have no side worth hearing. I'll give Travis two choices. He has five days to quit, or I'll fire him. If that happens the story will spread. Terry and their kids will see him for what he is. He'll never be allowed on company property again."

Rebekah trembled when he turned to her: "You'll have ten days. Pack your bags and load all your assets into trucks and get out. I'll have my Little Rock lawyers begin sorting out the myriad details involved in severing our connections. You'll deal with them about all that. Wesley will figure it out fast if you don't have the guts to tell him. I'm not sure what he'll do. That's between the two of you. Leave now because you have a lot of packing to do." Rebekah walked out with slow, sad steps.

When they heard the front door close Dumpling reacted: "You were awful. You didn't have to be that mean. Now what will they do?"

"Within five minutes they'll be on the phone figuring out how fast they can have a sit-down with you and get out of the mess they've made."

"What do you want me to do?"

"Your call. You're the peacemaker. I'm the warmaker. Come up with something tough, clear and workable. Their answer must be yes or no. No negotiations. They'll probably do anything you say to avoid me."

The now ex-lovers did what Ben expected. The next afternoon Dumpling and Ben sat at the kitchen table again. "Are you ready to hear what I worked out with them?"

"Yep."

"They agreed to the following: No personal relationship or intentional contact of any sort ever. None. They will never socialize or travel together for any reason.

Everything else stays the same. Both agreed and swore to God they would keep their word forever. I said if it happens again I'll tell Terry and Wesley everything. Then I'll turn it over to Connie. They're really scared. Is that enough?"

"We'll see."

"Ben, you're mad and got a right to be. But they're not bad people, just two good people who made a bad mistake. They're chock full of guilt. Rebekah cries and throws up when she thinks about it. Travis is beat to his knees with shame and can't look straight at you. They're too scared to face you. If my plan works, and I believe it will, don't let it end this way between the three of you. You've been Rebekah's special forever. Travis wants more than anything in life for you to respect him."

"So."

"Let me call Travis in the morning and ask him to come over here. After ya'll talk I'll call Rebekah with the same ask. But Ben, you got to work something out with 'em."

"Okay. Set it up."

When Travis shuffled in Ben kept it simple. "From this day forward we start over. Get it right this time and do exactly what you promised Dumpling."

"Yessir, I will. I swear to God I will. I'm so ashamed. It's all my fault."

"Do the math, Travis. Two persons fucking when they shouldn't be is never just one person's fault. Now you're a good man. Always remember that when you make decisions. That's the end of it. Now go."

Ben started before Rebekah could. "If you keep your word I'll keep mine. Don't throw up until after you leave."

"No. I'm not leaving until you listen to what I have to say. I know you can spare a few minutes for the village slut. What we did was inexcusable and had nothing to do with love. It was entirely physical and opportunistic on every level. I was as much at fault as Travis and will agonize for the rest of my life about the harm I've caused. I love Wesley, Benny and Bekah with all my heart. We have a good life. This is my home, my family, my calling. What was I thinking?"

"Can't help you there."

"How do the two of us get past this?"

"Don't know."

"What must I do?"

"Be who you say you are and keep your word."

"I will. I promise. What about Connie. She has avoided me for a couple of weeks."

"Face up to it. Tell her you know you fucked up as bad as bad gets. You're sorry. It will never happen again, and she has your word on it. If all that's true she'll know it. Getting past it in your mind will be tough. Memory Lane has potholes."

Dumpling interrupted: "Rebekah, never forget that you're kin, and we both love you. We'll stand with you till it all gets worked out."

"Ben, please help me hold it together."

"I will unless Wesley finds out and walks with the kids. I'll have to back him."

"I know that," Rebekah said wearily and ended the meeting.

Fortunately, Dumpling took point immediately. She found Connie and Cletis, and neither would throw the first stone. Donnalou began to take lunch to Rebekah's office for support and for someone to listen. The affair soon became bad history that nobody wanted to read.

Dumpling had become the county fixer and go-to for help with good ideas that needed a jump-start. She chaired a committee to identify promising students who needed money for college. They funded and managed the DHC scholarship program. Dumpling took Tuffy's place in the community and rarely turned anyone down who needed help. Folks knew Dumpling had Ben and kin behind her. Baptist Pharisees warmed to her after their preacher made Dumpling the church's budget chairman. Ben had offered to marry Dumpling. But she said they were married in their hearts so why complicate matters. That worked for many years until Wesley called for a sit-down.

Rebekah was behind it: "All of us know how much you love each other. You're married already in all the ways that count, except for the church and law. Right now I'll tell you one important reason we want you to marry. Benny and Bekah ask about it. I don't want to dodge it anymore by calling you life partners and being asked what that means. The two of you are the only real grans they have. I can't tell you how much we all love you and how safe that makes us feel. Wesley and I both are strongly for this so please make it formal and put it on the record."

"I asked, and she passed," Ben said.

"That's true," Dumpling responded "But it was a long time ago. Ben, I didn't know what would become of us then. I do now. I'm okay about it. But just the four of us with the kids and my preacher in the parlor. Short and simple. Those are my terms."

When Connie Came

Connie knocked twice and found them in Ben's office. "Dumpling, I'm sorry, but I need to talk to Ben alone."

Dumpling went upstairs, and Connie skipped the preface. "All of Preston's confiscated cash went to Mexican lawyers, cops, judges and officials. Gone forever. But it's a different story north of the border. The Feds couldn't find anything free and clear up here. Preston uses a bunch of corporations, trusts, limited partnerships and other things I don't understand. He's got a lot of money in a bunch of countries. Don't know yet where Langston is. Most of the time Preston stays in Monterrey with his slag Bonita. Several things we got to decide. I told you about the bad boys I put on the pad. Rough as gravel and pick up most everything goin' on around here. Even stuff that ain't here yet. I've been listening to them and some other sources. I held off with you because I wanted it nailed down. Right now I'm close as we're gonna get."

"Let's have it."

"You told me a guy close to Preston wanted to buy a piece of our land, and you said no."

"Yep. That ain't gonna happen. Preston would skin us for a scrap of bacon."

"Looks like he wants the whole hog. The Little Rock developer who bought the 80 that adjoins Dennis' and Pene's homeplace is frontin' Preston. The frontman hired ex-cons to start clearing up the 80 so Preston can build a mansion. They're also Preston's muscle and handle the U.S. side of his drug empire with Tio. Now the developer is pushing everybody northwest of town near Dennis to sell. It's get out of the way or get runover."

"Cletis told me Dennis' cattle have been dying with no sign of why," Ben said. "Now we know why."

"That's right. Pene is worried because their kids are workin' the operation. Dennis told me somebody almost ran one of them off the road one night. Dennis has heart troubles. He's not able to take on Preston and those cutthroats."

"That changes the rules then. Where is Preston now?"

"Shacked up in Mexico. We're talkin' about this because I don't know what you want me to do."

"It's not our problem yet, but it will be. Pene's family is well off, but the real wealth and power around here belongs to us. Ultimately Preston will come after us. Ideas?"

"Yeah, but you may not like 'em."

"Try me."

"Private contractor. You remember Lee, who helped us stop Smiley. We've stayed close over the years."

"Define close."

"Too close to talk to you about it."

"I'll be damned. That explains your frequent mysterious trips. Where do you meet?"

"None of your business."

"If this has been going on for years why don't ya'll go public?"

"He's black, Ben. You know what our people think about that. We plan to do more later, but right now we keep an apartment in Fayetteville near the university. Black and white folks together around there don't get looks. Now all this stays between us, right?"

"Right. And ya'll together are a good thing."

"That's for sure, because right now we got some bad business to do. I told Lee we want Preston gone for good and all his cronies in the county. We'll scrape up leftovers. I gave him details so he could give me a price. It's not gonna be cheap, but he says it's doable with enough lead time. I told him we'd need your nod before startin'."

"You and Lee handle it. My primary concern is that we do it all at once and completely. Run the table. I want all of Preston's good stuff after we're done, including his interest in the Oklahoma casino Leon told me about. Turn it into a financial windfall to cover the cost and risk."

"What else you thinkin'?"

"The county sheriff's granddaughter just died of an overdose from local crack. Paul Huggins is way past unhappy. His wife is emotionally destroyed. I know him from favors. He trusts me. Let me circle some wagons before you start."

"I'll tell Lee."

Ben waited on a plank bench by the sheriff's front door early in the morning. Sheriff Huggins saw him from the window and opened the door. "You comin' in, or am I comin' out?"

"Best you come out."

"Okay. With coffee or bourbon?"

"Black coffee."

The sheriff returned with the coffee and sat at the far end of the plank. "This ain't good news, is it?"

"Could be. Sorry about your granddaughter. Is anybody up for it?"

"Nope. Nobody heard, saw or remembers a thing."

"What the hell is going on around here, Paul?"

"Bad men are running the show. They got more men, money, lawyers and guns than we got. Law can't stop 'em."

"What if someone else stopped them?"

"Who?"

"Somebody who can."

"How?"

"If nobody cooks, sells or smuggles in this county that would stop a lot of crime and sorrow."

"Reckon it would, but what exactly are you talking about?"

"I'm talking about a clean county where kids don't die like she did." Ben nodded, put his cup on the bench and drove off to avoid follow-up questions.

"Lee is on it," Connie said. "He's dealt with bad guys like them all his life. Me and him agree that our system don't work anymore. Judges make rich men pay a little when they hurt people. But that don't hurt rich men. Judges bail out rapists and robbers, and they keep raping and robbing. Hard cases ain't ever gonna change. They just scam the system with sleazy lawyers. Lee says you got to kill bad men to stop the problems they cause. That's the only thing that works. I agree with him."

"I don't disagree. But let's not get enthusiastic."

"Lee says what happens to Preston will happen in Mexico. Apparently there ain't many honest officials in the country. Lee's people down there will arrange that. Preston's people up here are low-lifes. They'll have an accident, and nobody will care. What do you want to do with Tio? He manages all the smugglers, cookers and dealers around here."

"I want a sit-down with him after the fireworks. Where is he?"

"He goes back and forth. Lee's people will find him."

The barn on Preston's property blew up with most of his criminal hired help in it. The crew had been drinking whiskey and smoking reefer during an all-night poker game when a faulty gas line exploded, according to the county sheriff's report. The building and everything near it disintegrated when adjoining diesel tanks exploded. The next morning, after Preston got the phone call in Monterrey, his driver dropped him off at the local airport. He boarded a helicopter for a run to Mexico City where his jet waited. He never made it. The chopper went down after a rotor malfunction and crashed in a pasture. The explosion killed everyone on board and two grazing cows.

Pene's Thoughts

Dennis went to Little Rock for heart bypass surgery, and Ben showed up. In the waiting room he saw Pene and her Marine Corps son Jeffrey. He looked straight, stiff and serious. She walked over. Her son followed.

Pene gave Ben a half-hug. "Thanks so much for coming. I didn't expect this."

"How is Dennis doing?"

"Everything is going well. Apparently bypasses aren't such a big deal anymore. Ben, this is Jeffrey." They shook hands. "I appreciate you coming for another reason. Can we talk?"

"Sure. Here?"

"No, privately. Let's sit by the nearest exit."

They sat in shade furnished by a Japanese maple. "So?" Ben prompted.

"I have a few questions."

"Ask."

"A Little Rock developer came to Dennis' house a couple of days after Preston and his outlaws died. I'm staying here to help with everything. The guy was a nervous wreck. Apologized profusely for having asked Dennis to sell some of our land to him during our difficulties. The man kept saying all would be well from here on. It was strange. What do you think about that?"

"Never knew about it. So never thought about it. Not thinking about it now."

"Wow. That's slippery. Haven't seen that in years. But I remember it from the old days."

"What else you got?"

"Not too long before the explosion Connie saw Dennis in Dotty's. She told him not to worry. Things would come out okay. Dennis thought Connie was trying to cheer him up. With hindsight it could have meant more than that."

"Ask Connie."

"Ben, the whole county is convinced Connie was involved in this. But everyone knows you call all the shots. It's clear my family benefited from what happened. That puts me in the frame. A lot of people died. I want to know if they were killed because of my family."

Pene's son had been watching from a window and noticed his mother's frustration. He marched out. "Is everything okay out here?"

Ben: "Why wouldn't it be?"

"Mom looks uncomfortable."

"She believes I'm a serial killer and is irritated because I won't confess and be executed."

"Ben, Jeffrey is worried that now you might want our land and businesses."

"Both of you take a close look and tell me if you think I need another fucking problem in my life." They did and saw he didn't. "Pene, leave me the hell alone forever. Just tell Dennis I showed up and wish him well."

The county sheriff called Ben early in the morning and asked him to drop by. Ben sat on the bench, and Huggins opened the front door holding two cups of black coffee.

Ben said, "This ain't good news is it?"

"Nope. It's about Pene. She's still fussing about the explosion at Preston's barn. The one that killed Preston's outlaws. The gas heater exploded in the barn office. The fuel tanks blew and wiped out the place. We ruled it an accident that started with a gas leak. She says it wasn't properly investigated. I told her there were body parts and crap strung out over forty acres. Bits and pieces everywhere. My deputy Shorty found places where rats had been gnawing on the lines. The dead bastards had been doping in there all night and were stumbling drunk.

"That's about all we had to investigate. I told the state police colonel about it, and he said good enough. But somehow it ain't good enough for Pene. After Preston died in the helicopter crash, she wants to tie it all together and go after somebody. Now she's way up the colonel's ass about it. She wants him to spend a fortune the state ain't got on an investigation with the FBI about the whole thing. I talked to them, too, and all of us want her to shut up and go away. You got any ideas about how we get that done?"

"I may," Ben said and finished his coffee.

Jeffrey met Ben at a picnic table in the town's public park where hillbilly kids tried to play soccer with rules they couldn't figure out. The morning sun had not yet warmed the wooden seats or the Marine's expression. "What do you want?" he said.

"Need to talk to you about your mother."

"Why not talk to her?"

"Your Uncle Dennis once told me Pene was too bull-headed to change her mind even when wrong. I found that to be true."

"What's your point?"

"You've seen bad things happen in combat. You know about special operations people and how good they are. So you might help me with several concerns. Pene is obsessed with what happened here and in Mexico that took down viscous killers who were torturing and murdering innocents. I'm not sure why. But she is pestering the county sheriff and state police about what authorities have officially ruled accidents. I assume she believes they weren't accidents but done by people for unknown reasons. If she is correct, these people would have to be extraordinarily competent and probably ex-military. Their planning, precision, reach and resources are remarkable."

"She only wants the truth."

"But what if there ain't no truth to be had except this. If Pene is correct, the people she suspects wouldn't tolerate for long anyone attempting to expose them, would they? You may know and have worked with men just like them. Would they?"

"Probably not."

"If Pene is right, you know what's coming if she continues. My concern is that you can stop her but may not. Now put an end to all this for your family's sake."

Tio and Butch

Tio lived because Ben needed a sit-down. Lee's men found him at a posh Little Rock restaurant with a lovely young mistress. They let her go and stowed him in a hideaway house. Tio knew Preston was dead and his crews had been decimated. But he seemed unperturbed.

Ben sat opposite him. "What you have to do is take my county off your map. No cooking, selling, importing, smuggling, nothing. The rest of the world is yours. If you do that you live. If not, you die. Pass along to your associates that anyone committing violent crime in my county will be gutted and burned. No cops. No lawyers. No courts. No excuses."

"Deal," Tio said. He stood: "Need my truck keys." Though stunned by his abruptness, Ben let Tio drive away.

Ben's meeting with Butch Miller took longer. Connie came with him to ensure it lasted long enough to suit her. She started talking while Ben and Dumpling observed from the couch. "I figure ya'll have seen Butch around here. He grew up on Knothead Road with some brothers who probably gave the road its name. I had to lock and load on two of 'em."

Butch laughed: "That's when Kirby and Porky tried to steal Connie's truck with her sleeping in it."

"I can't believe you are related to those two mutts," Connie said. "Anyhow, tell 'em your story."

"I graduated from high school here and went into the Marines when I was 18. Made rank and recon. Did special ops with the Corps until a federal agency paid me a large bonus to cross over and develop aggressive security activities in several countries with more sand than Grinder's Switch."

"What about training and education," Ben said.

"American University over there for two years. Foreign language courses of no use here. High-tech communications and surveillance training. Electronics, satellites. Classified spook stuff. Combat and weapons training from the Corps."

"Why are we here?" Ben asked. But he already knew the answer.

"I want your approval for Butch to replace me," Connie said. "Plus, make sure you and Dumpling have more than enough personal security. I told Butch you can be aggravating but to pay attention. There's a lot to be learned. Butch knows Wesley is the chair now, and he signed off on him taking my place. Butch has promised me and Wesley that he'll see to your safety. We upset apple carts from here to Mexico City. Tio says another cartel has people in Little Rock now and is heading north. He's concerned about having enough dependable men to keep his word to you. Tio says the drug cartels know we're their problem around here. Lee has two top guns ridin' shotgun with me for the time being. Who knows? Now that we got casino cash rolling in the Italians may show up wantin' points. Wesley, Lee and me asked Butch to set up a high-tech intelligence and surveillance network. I told all of 'em at the sit-down that I can't keep track of all this shit anymore so thank God we got Butch on board. Are you all good?"

"Yep."

Dumpling cleared her throat softly, but all three noticed. "I wonder," she said to Butch, "why you came back here after such an important career?"

"It was that career or my family. R. J. --that's my wife Rhonda Jo--flew to Dubai with our two girls after I got an offer to fill a permanent position there. For a week she watched how women and girls are mistreated. R. J. is a feisty redhead from here. I could tell right away she was going to get into it with somebody important. I couldn't protect her there. We came home to raise our girls here. I work with my brothers in our logging operation and do some gray work off the grid. I helped one of Lee's men in Lebanon when he got in a bad jam back in the day. In our world memories are long and word gets around. I'm glad to be part of what you're doing. I'm a man of my word."

"I believe you are," Ben said, relieved that he could let go of a lot of stuff now.

Last Canto

Ben often tugged on mental threads that led nowhere. Thoughts fell away mid-sentence. Names dodged his porous recall. Words evaporated on the tongue. Fortunately, Wesley now ran it all with his people. Ben sensed his time soon would stop altogether. Dumpling prayed for him incessantly. But Ben worried because the clockmaker may have kept score, including the minuses. Still, looking back he was satisfied. He knew there was some truth in the madness.

The Author

Van Hawkins was raised in a farming family in the Missouri Bootheel, where land, work and story were inseparable. He holds a bachelor's degree in literature from the University of Missouri, along with master's degrees in pastoral counseling from Loyola University in New Orleans and heritage studies from Arkansas State University.

He is a former art critic, feature writer and city editor at the *Newport News Times Herald* in Tidewater Virginia. This is his 13th book. They all tell stories about the South, its people, places, problems and possibilities.

In 2025, he received the American Legacy Book Award in Anthologies–Non-Fiction for *Cries from the Walls: Hell in Arkansas Prisons*. The work is a collection of rare firsthand accounts and historical documents concerning atrocities in Arkansas prisons. He also was a finalist in General History, Military History, and Southern History categories.

His work reflects a sustained interest in power, justice, heritage, and the enduring structures that shape Southern life — themes that resonate deeply in *Hillbilly Godfather*.